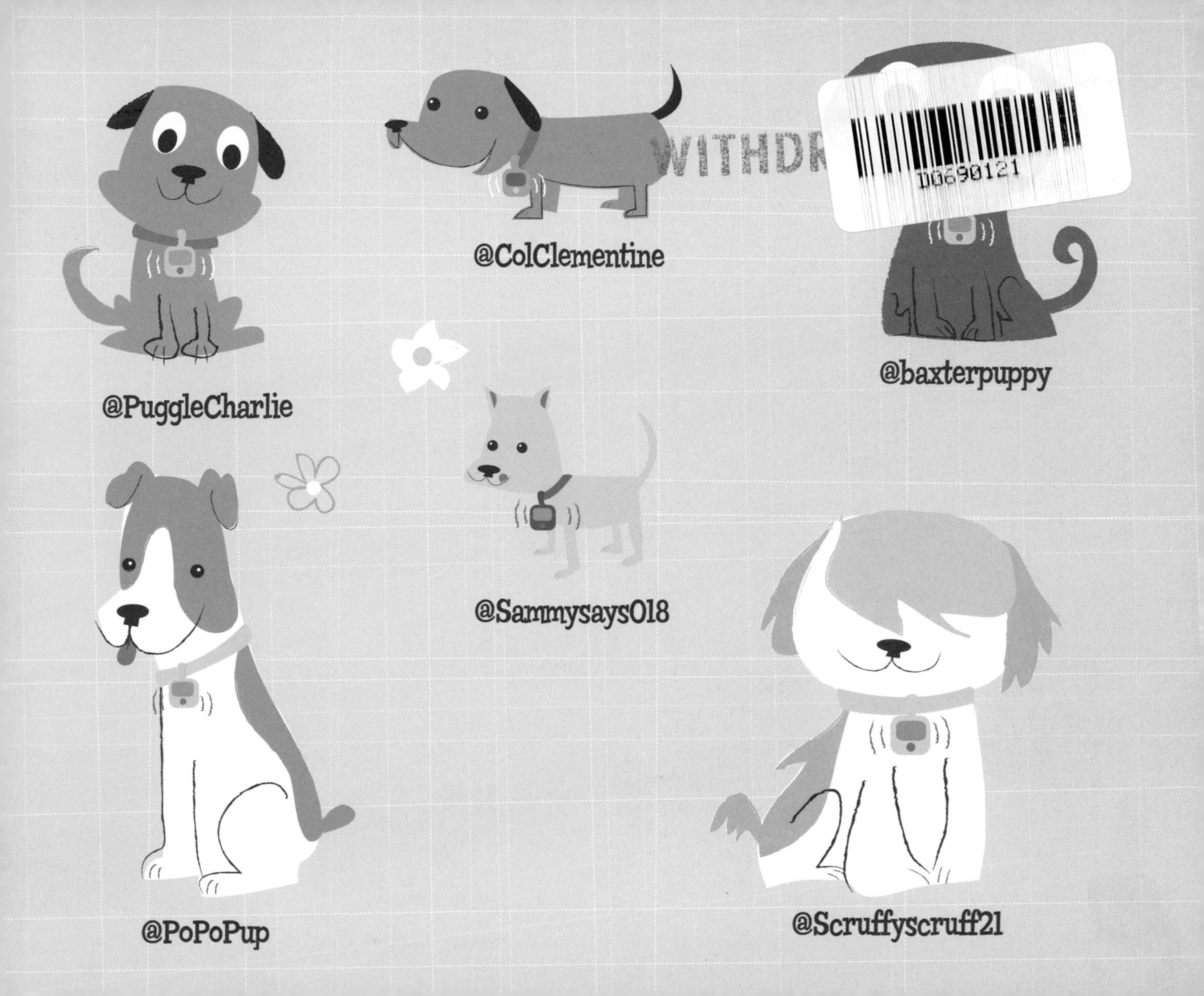
@PuggleCharlie
@ColClementine
@baxterpuppy
@Sammysays018
@PoPoPup
@Scruffyscruff21

For Baxter Blue Cheese, and
with thanks and love to Mike and Avery—D.M.

Copyright © 2012 Doreen Marts
BalloonToons™ is a registered
trademark of Harriet Ziefert, Inc.
All rights reserved/CIP data is available.
Published in the United States 2012 by
🍎 Blue Apple Books
515 Valley Street, Maplewood, NJ 07040
www.blueapplebooks.com
First Edition
Printed in China 05/12
HC ISBN: 978-1-60905-199-0
2 4 6 8 10 9 7 5 3 1
PB ISBN: 978-1-60905-200-3
2 4 6 8 10 9 7 5 3 1

BAXTER THE TWEETING DOG

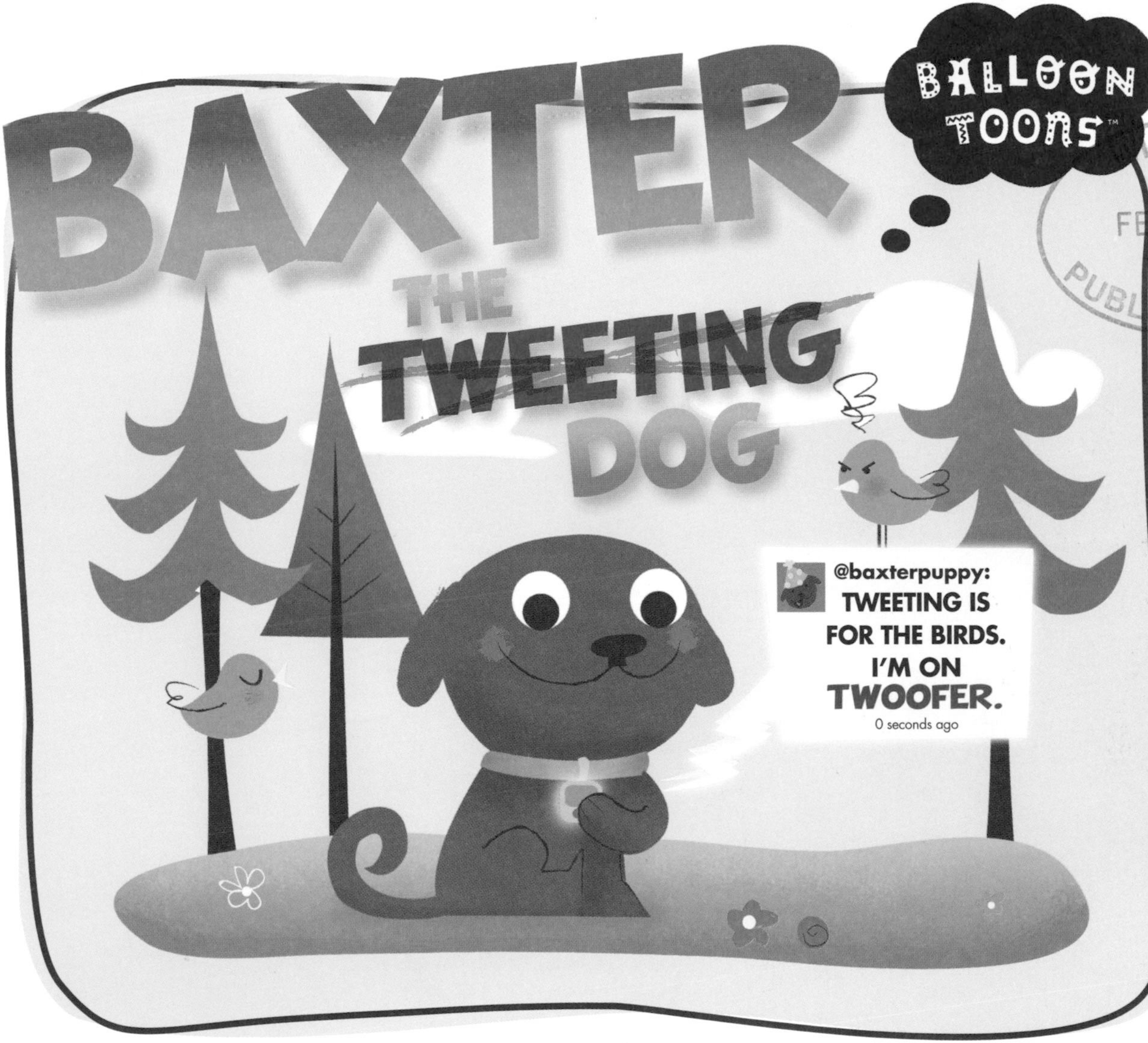
BALLOON TOONS™
@baxterpuppy:
TWEETING IS FOR THE BIRDS. I'M ON TWOFER.
0 seconds ago

BLUE APPLE

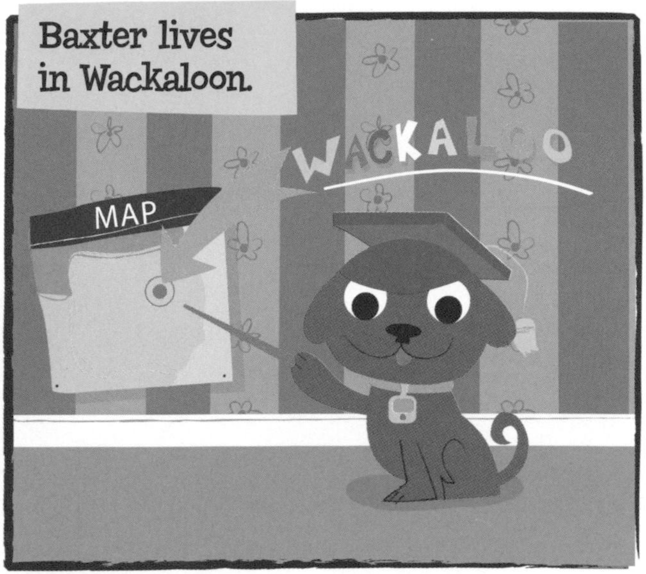
Baxter lives in Wackaloon.
MAP

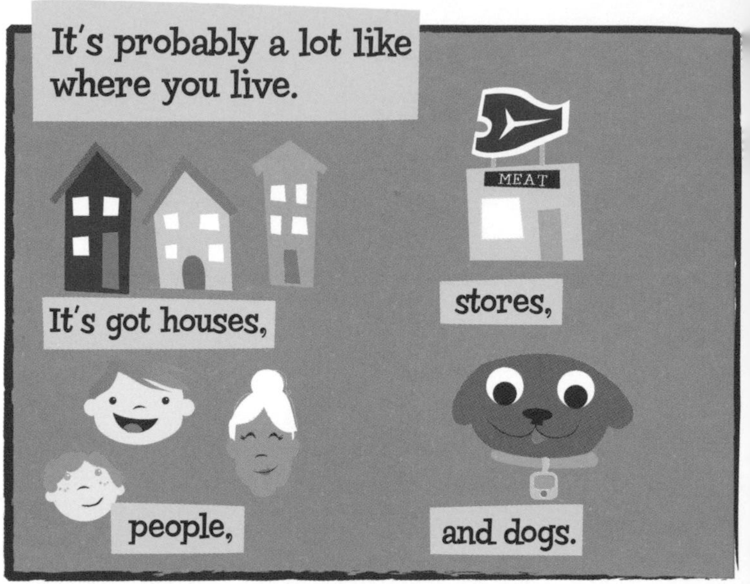
It's probably a lot like where you live.
MEAT
It's got houses,
stores,
people,
and dogs.

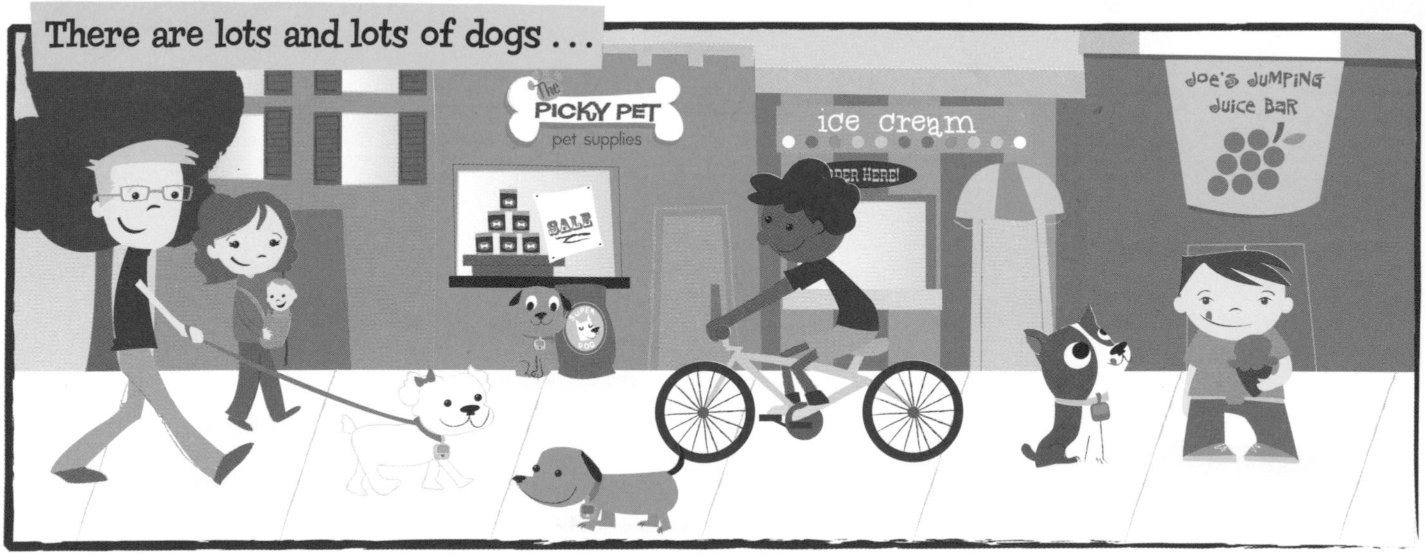
There are lots and lots of dogs . . .
The PICKY PET
pet supplies
SALE
ice cream
Joe's Jumping Juice Bar

and a little something else called:

TWOOFER.

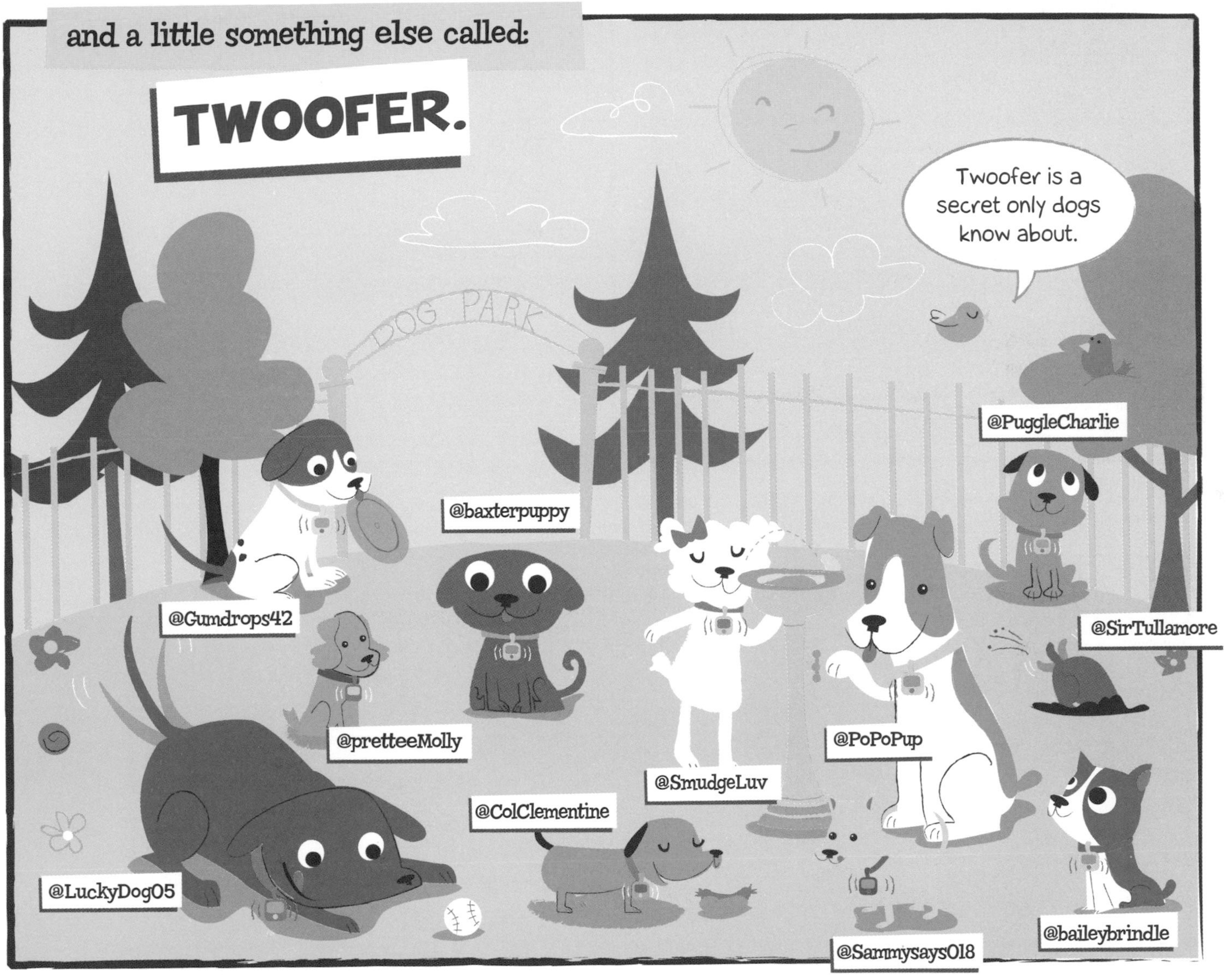
DOG PARK
Twoofer is a secret only dogs know about.
@PuggleCharlie
@baxterpuppy
@Gumdrops42
@SirTullamore
@pretteeMolly
@PoPoPup
@SmudgeLuv
@ColClementine
@LuckyDog05
@baileybrindle
@Sammysays018

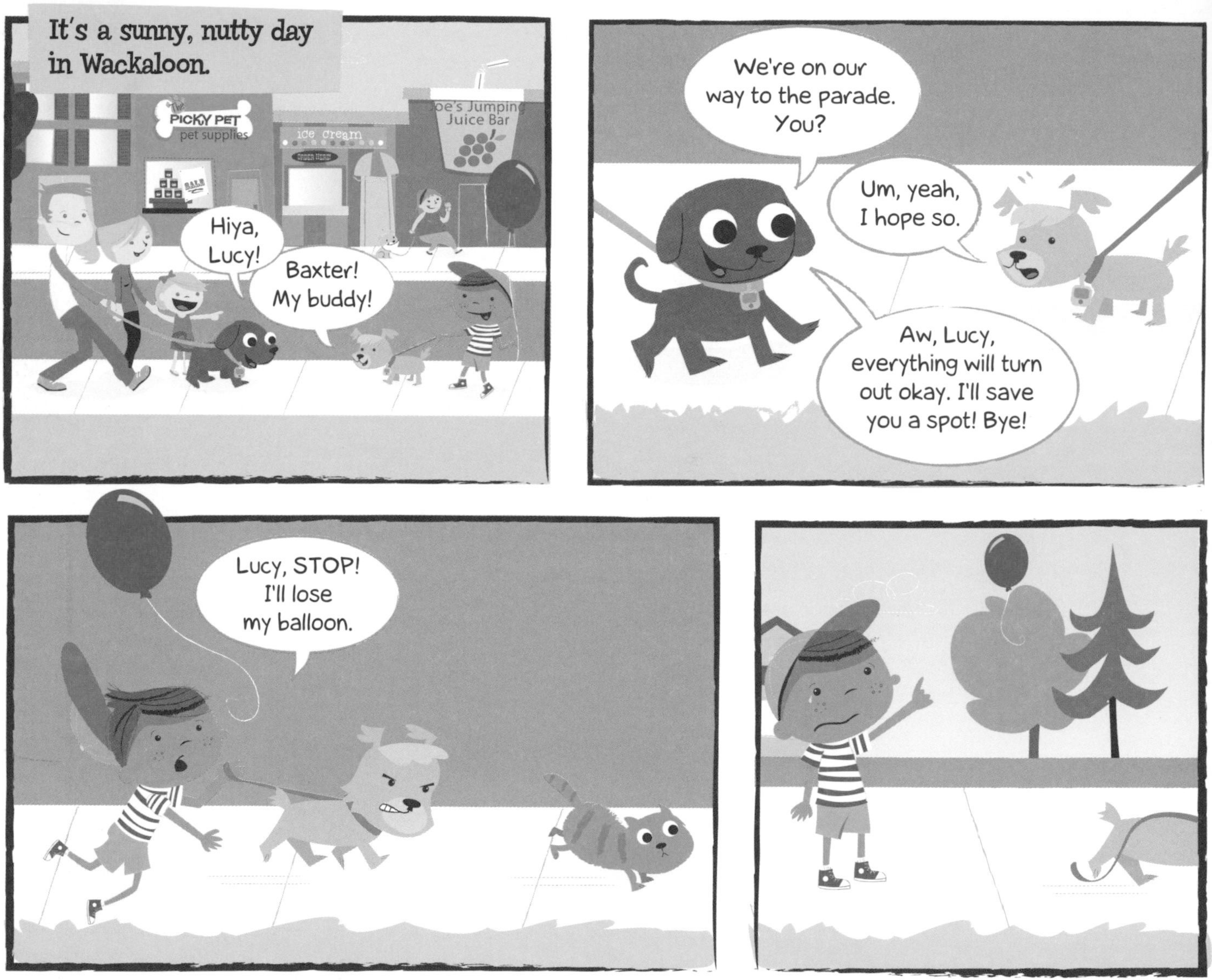
It's a sunny, nutty day in Wackaloon.
PICKY PET
pet supplies
ice cream
Juice Bar
Hiya, Lucy!
Baxter! My buddy!
We're on our way to the parade. You?
Um, yeah, I hope so.
Aw, Lucy, everything will turn out okay. I'll save you a spot! Bye!
Lucy, STOP! I'll lose my balloon.

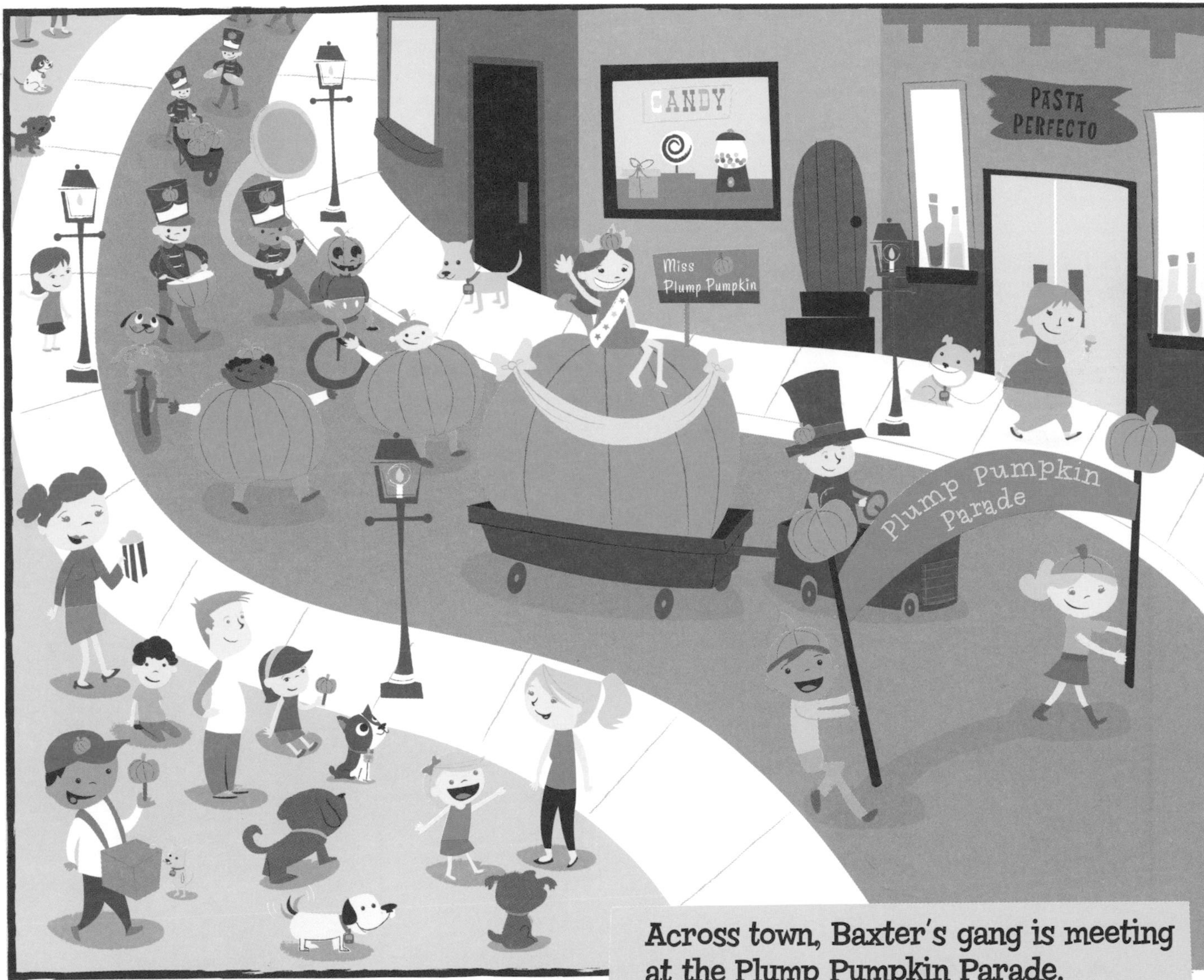
CANDY
PASTA PERFECTO
Miss Plump Pumpkin
Plump Pumpkin Parade

Across town, Baxter's gang is meeting at the Plump Pumpkin Parade.

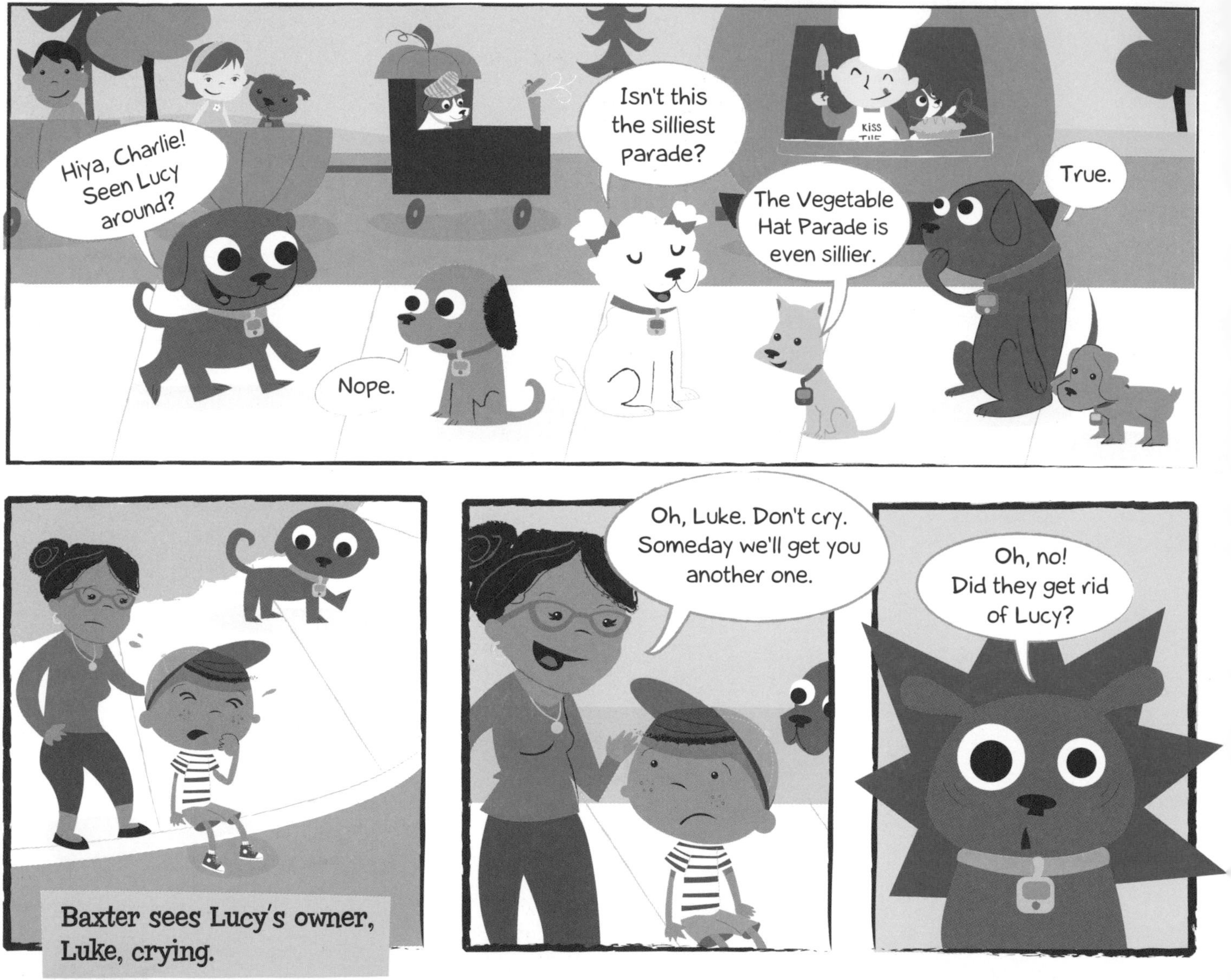
Hiya, Charlie! Seen Lucy around?
Nope.
Isn't this the silliest parade?
The Vegetable Hat Parade is even sillier.
True.
Baxter sees Lucy's owner, Luke, crying.
Oh, Luke. Don't cry. Someday we'll get you another one.
Oh, no! Did they get rid of Lucy?

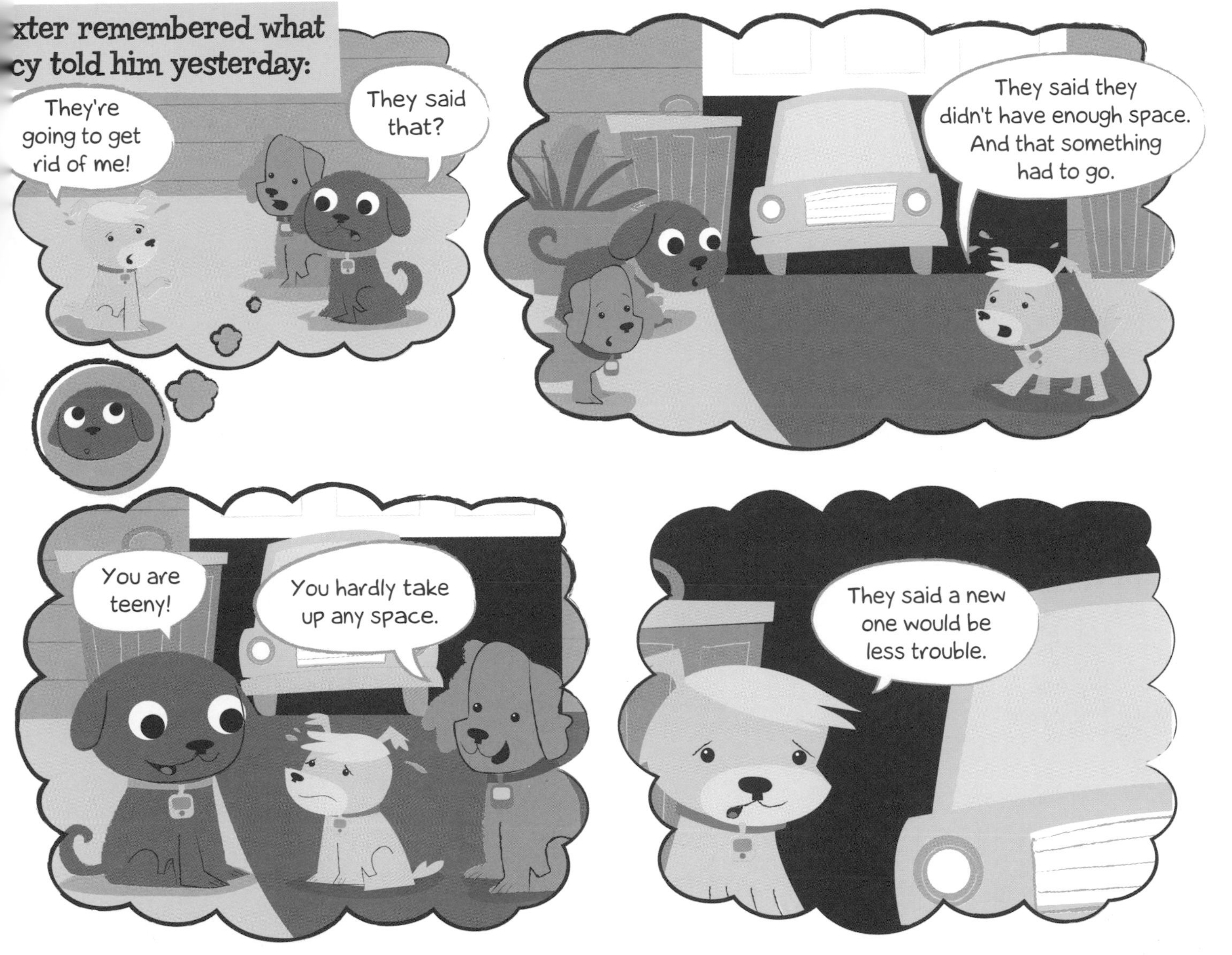
xter remembered what
cy told him yesterday:
They're going to get rid of me!
They said that?
They said they didn't have enough space. And that something had to go.
You are teeny!
You hardly take up any space.
They said a new one would be less trouble.

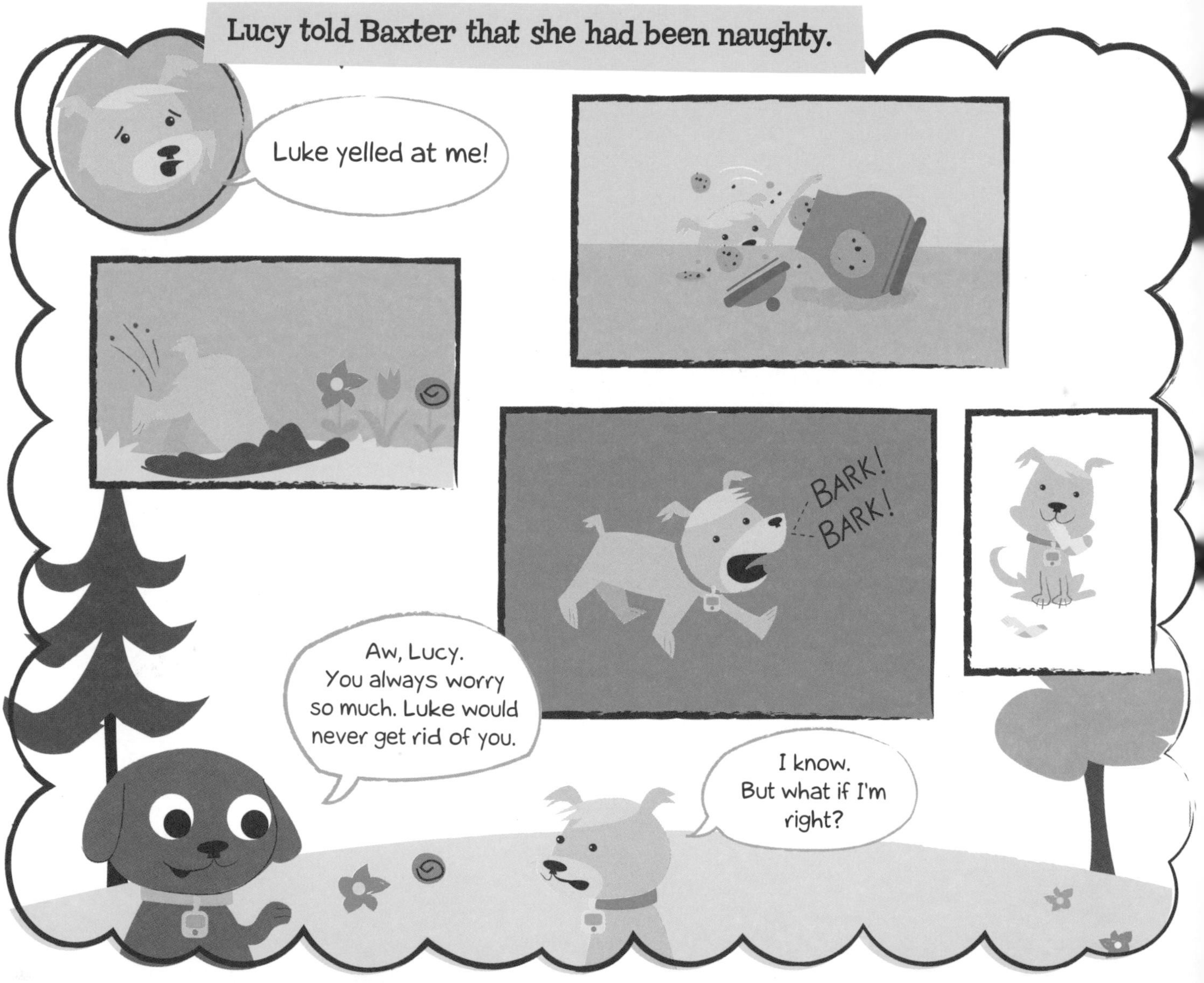
Lucy told Baxter that she had been naughty.
Luke yelled at me!
BARK! BARK!
Aw, Lucy. You always worry so much. Luke would never get rid of you.
I know. But what if I'm right?

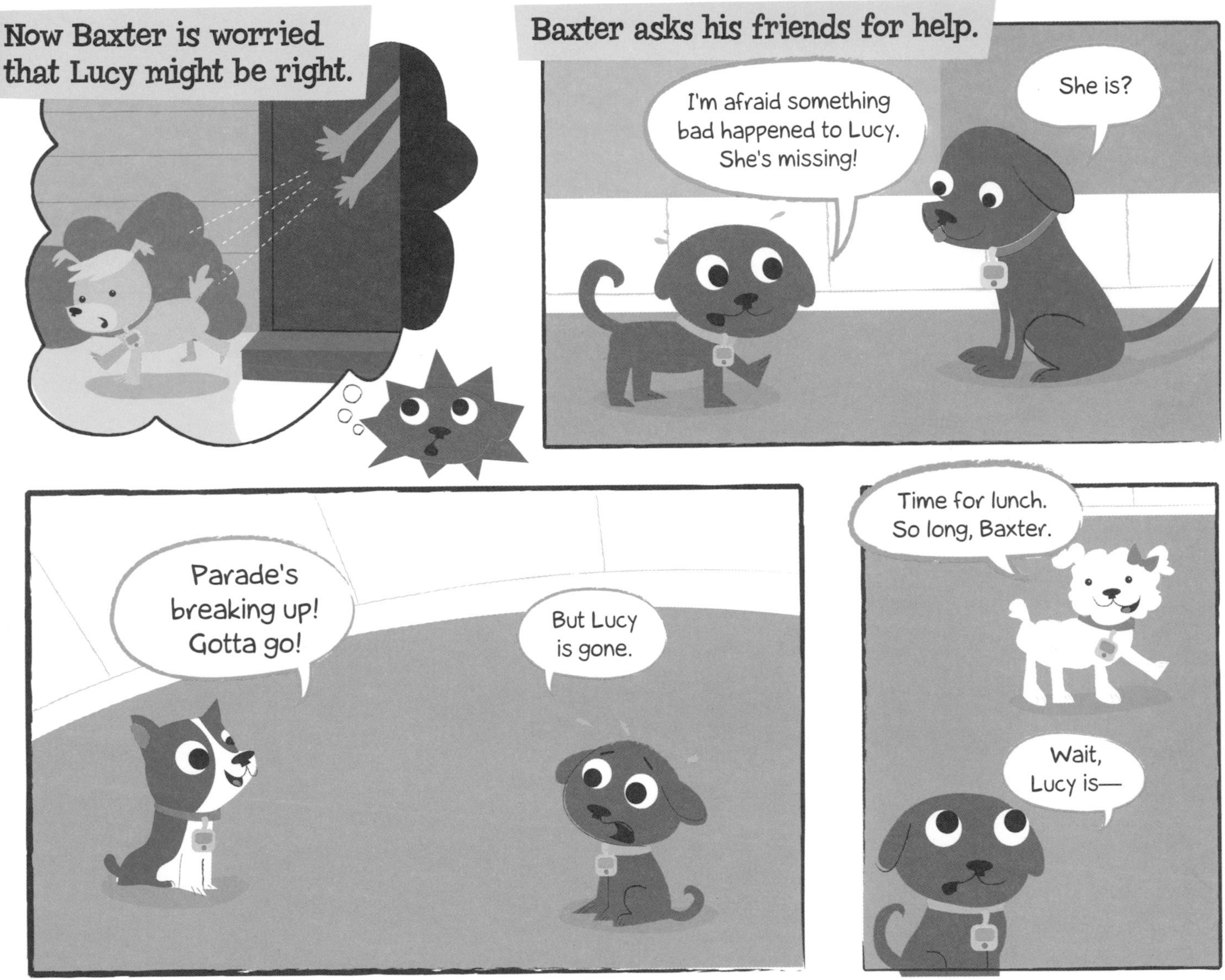
Now Baxter is worried that Lucy might be right.
Baxter asks his friends for help.
I'm afraid something bad happened to Lucy. She's missing!
She is?
Parade's breaking up! Gotta go!
But Lucy is gone.
Time for lunch. So long, Baxter.
Wait, Lucy is—

Baxter's friends all have other plans.

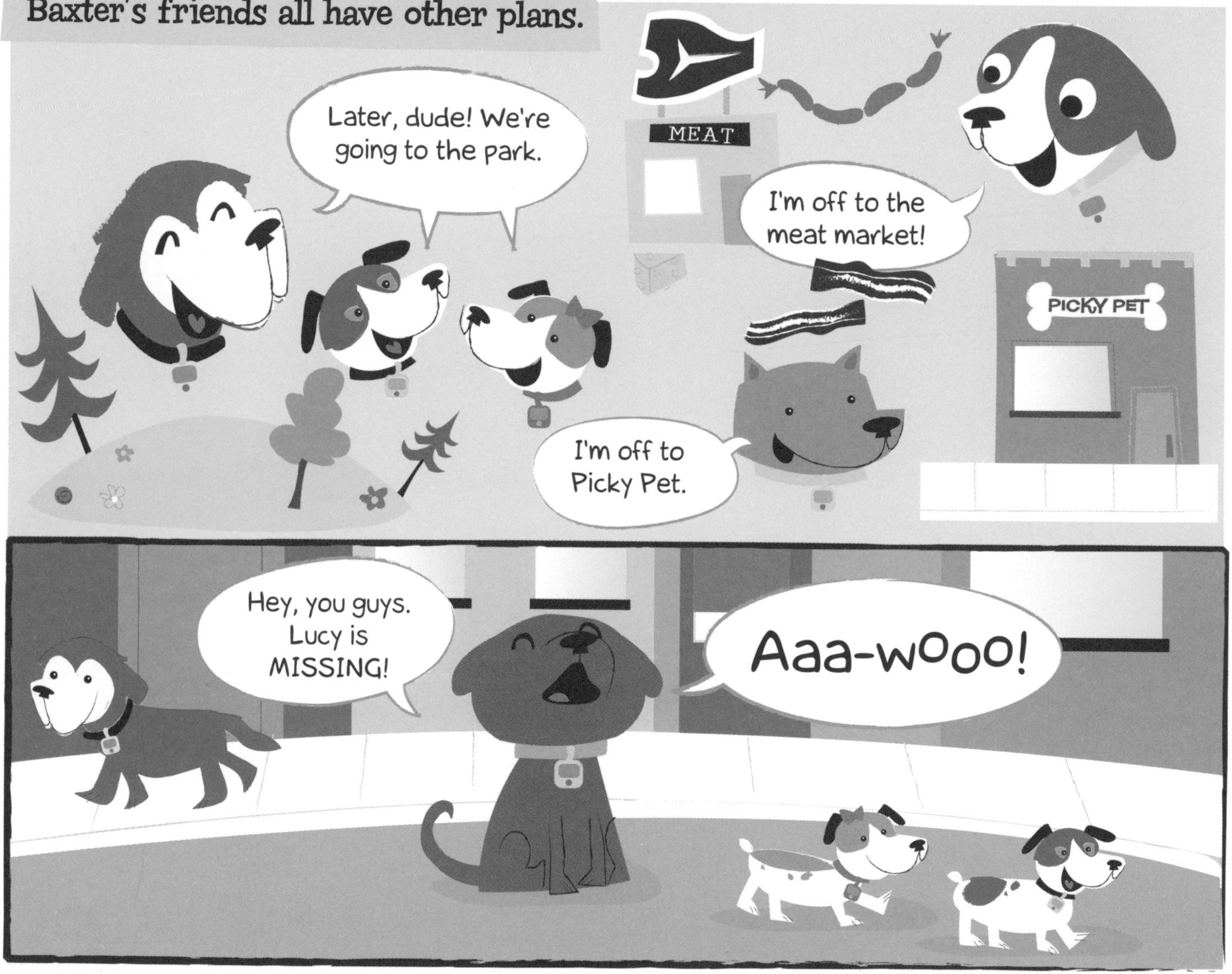
MEAT
Later, dude! We're going to the park.
I'm off to the meat market!
PICKY PET
I'm off to Picky Pet.
Hey, you guys. Lucy is MISSING!
Aaa-wooo!

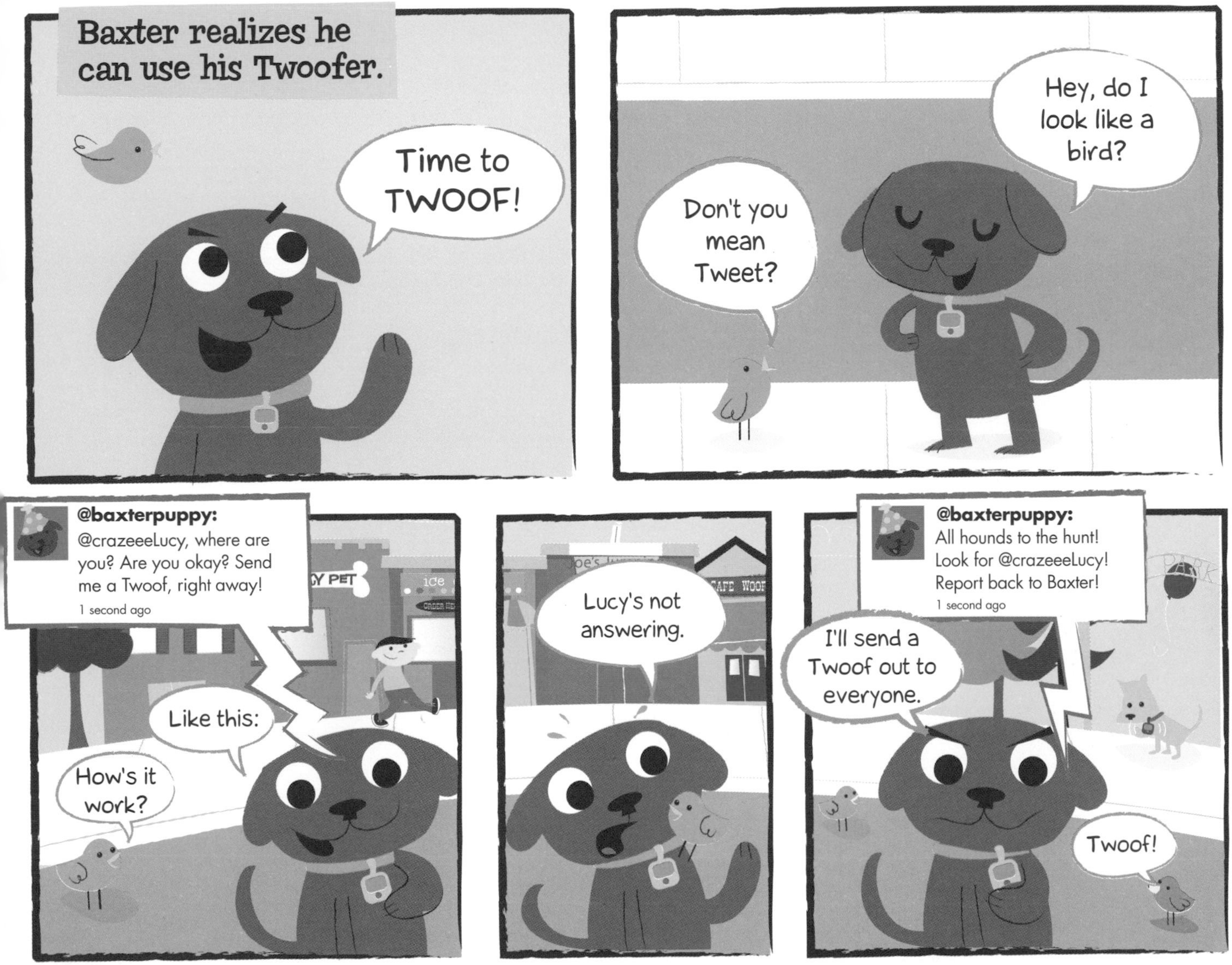
Baxter realizes he can use his Twoofer.
Time to TWOOF!
Hey, do I look like a bird?
Don't you mean Tweet?
@baxterpuppy:
@crazeeeLucy, where are you? Are you okay? Send me a Twoof, right away!
1 second ago
How's it work?
Like this:
Lucy's not answering.
@baxterpuppy:
All hounds to the hunt! Look for @crazeeeLucy! Report back to Baxter!
1 second ago
I'll send a Twoof out to everyone.
Twoof!

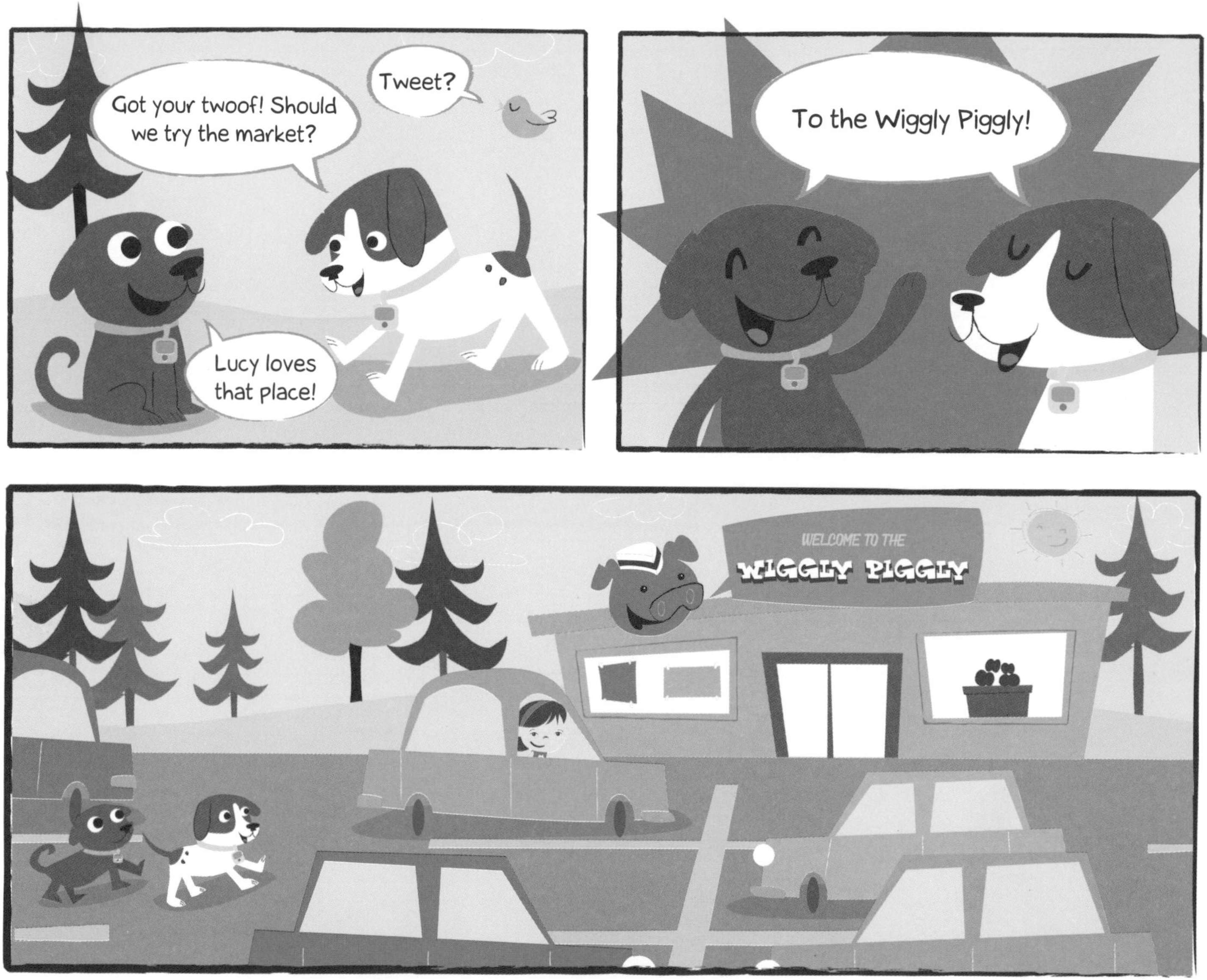
Got your twoof! Should we try the market?
Tweet?
Lucy loves that place!
To the Wiggly Piggly!
WELCOME TO THE
WIGGLY PIGGLY

Baxter and his pals search all over the market for Lucy.

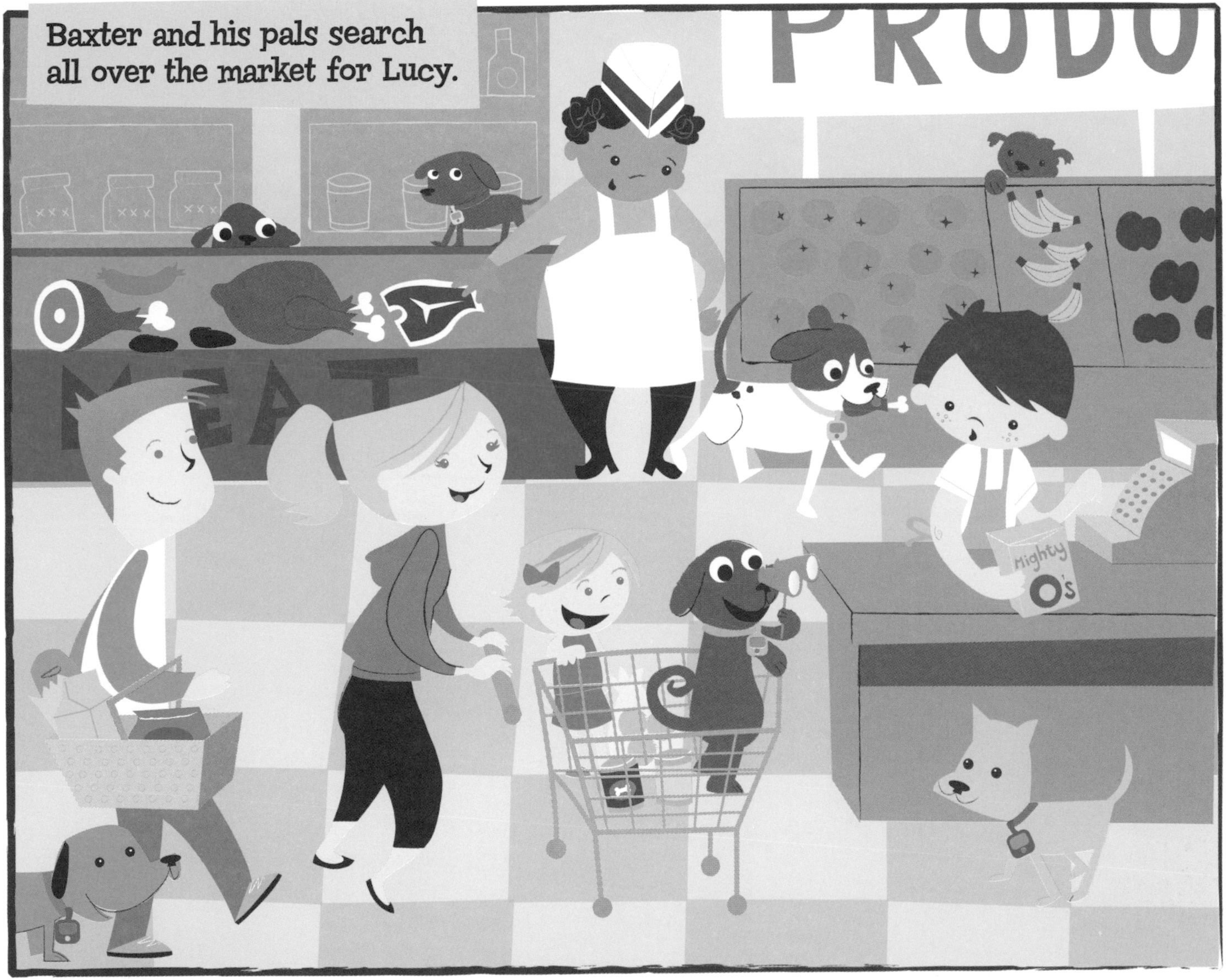
PRODU
MEAT
Mighty
O's

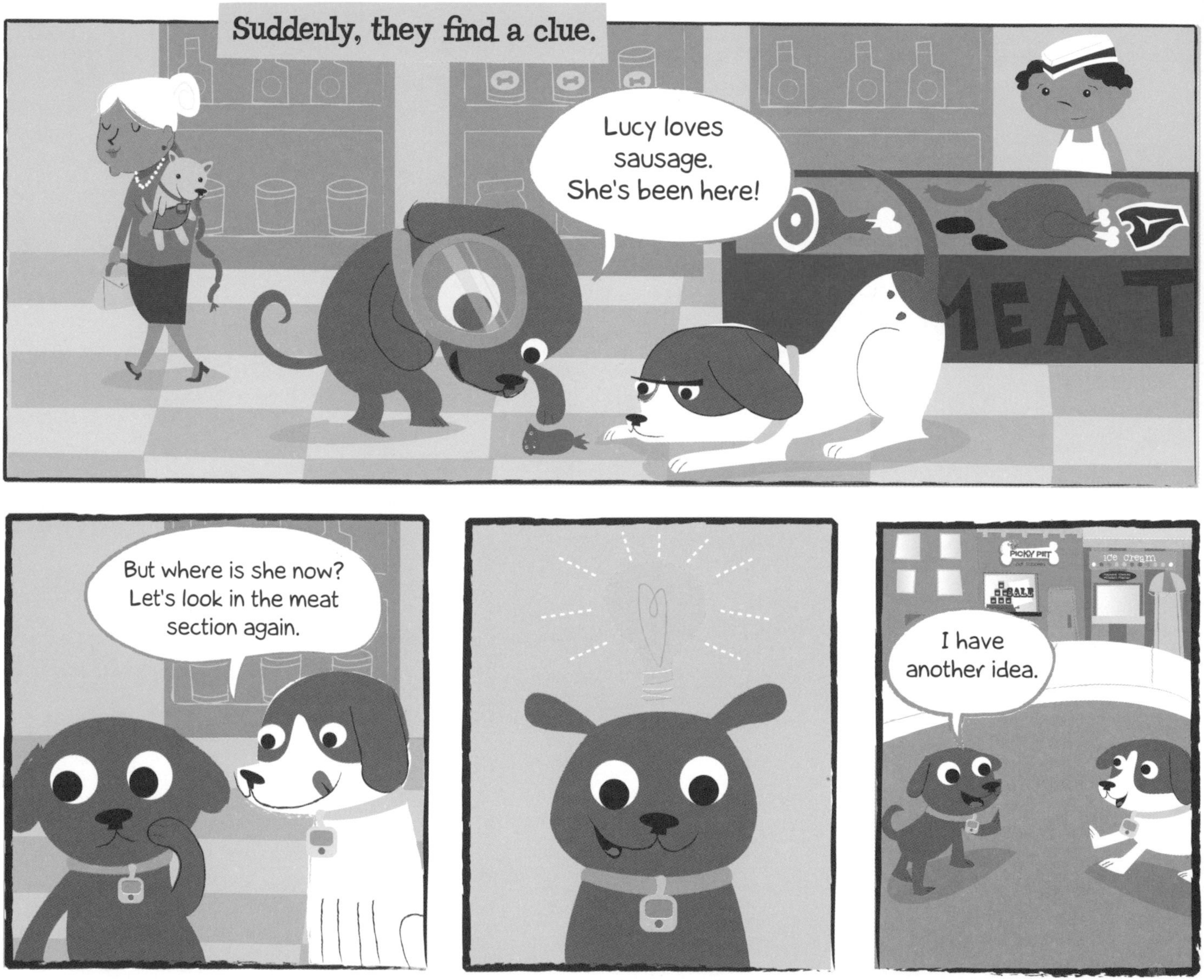
Suddenly, they find a clue.
Lucy loves sausage. She's been here!
MEAT
But where is she now? Let's look in the meat section again.
PICKY PET
ice cream
I have another idea.

Baxter leads his pals to the Picky Pet store.

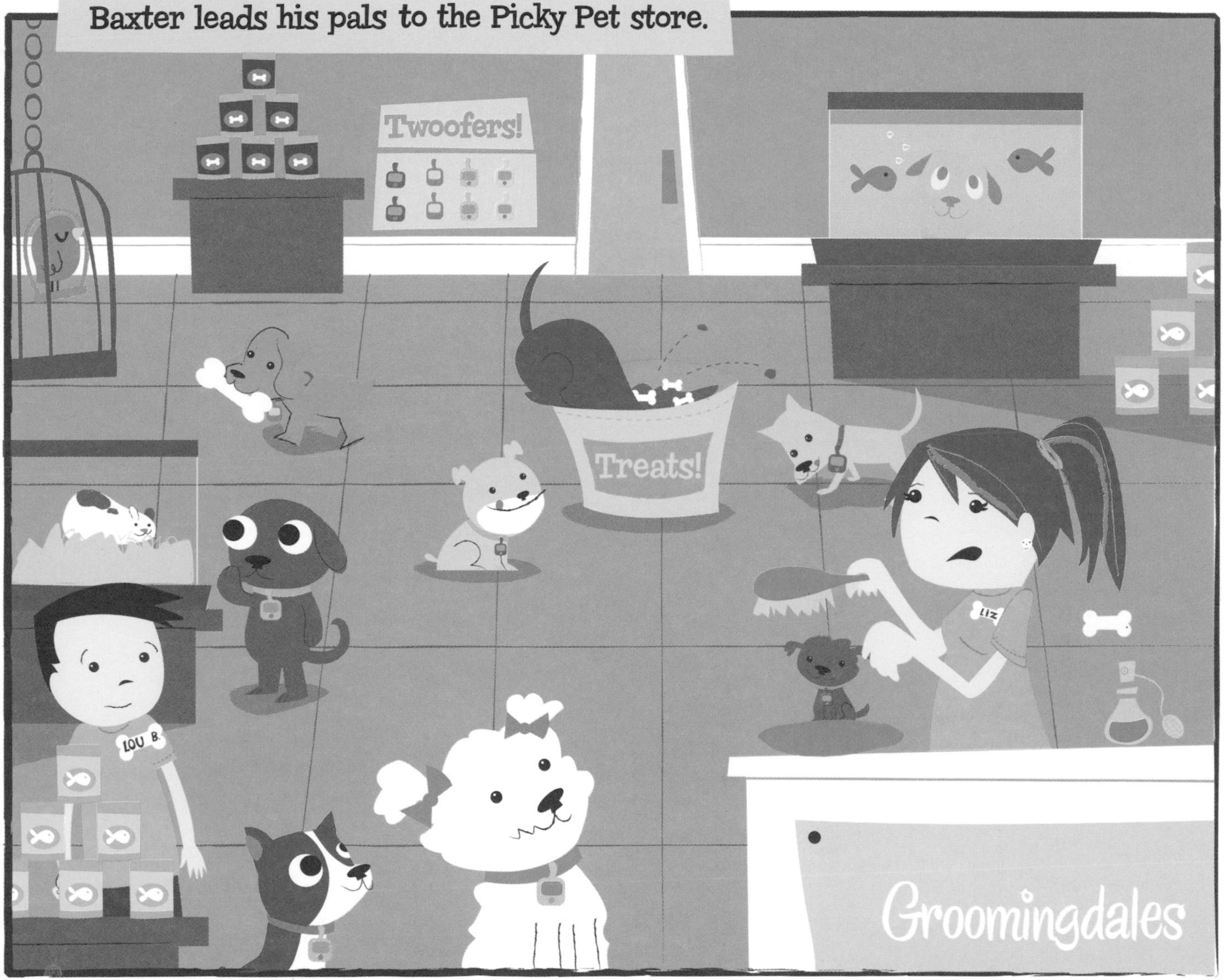
Twoofers!
Treats!
LOU B.
LIZ
Groomingdales

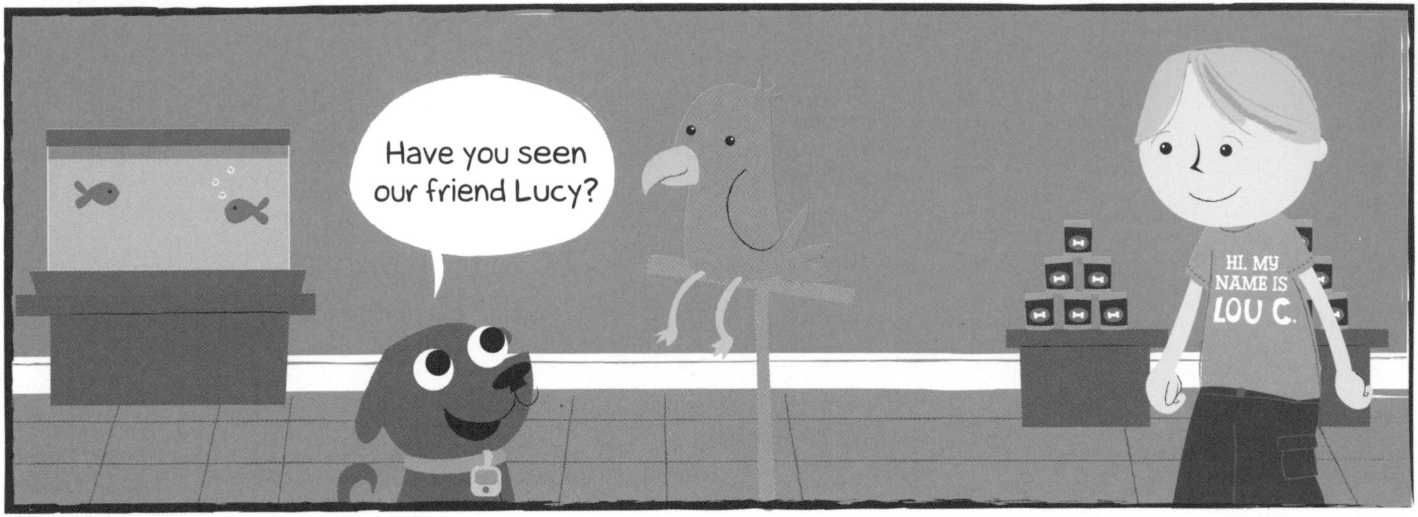
Have you seen our friend Lucy?
HI. MY NAME IS LOU C.

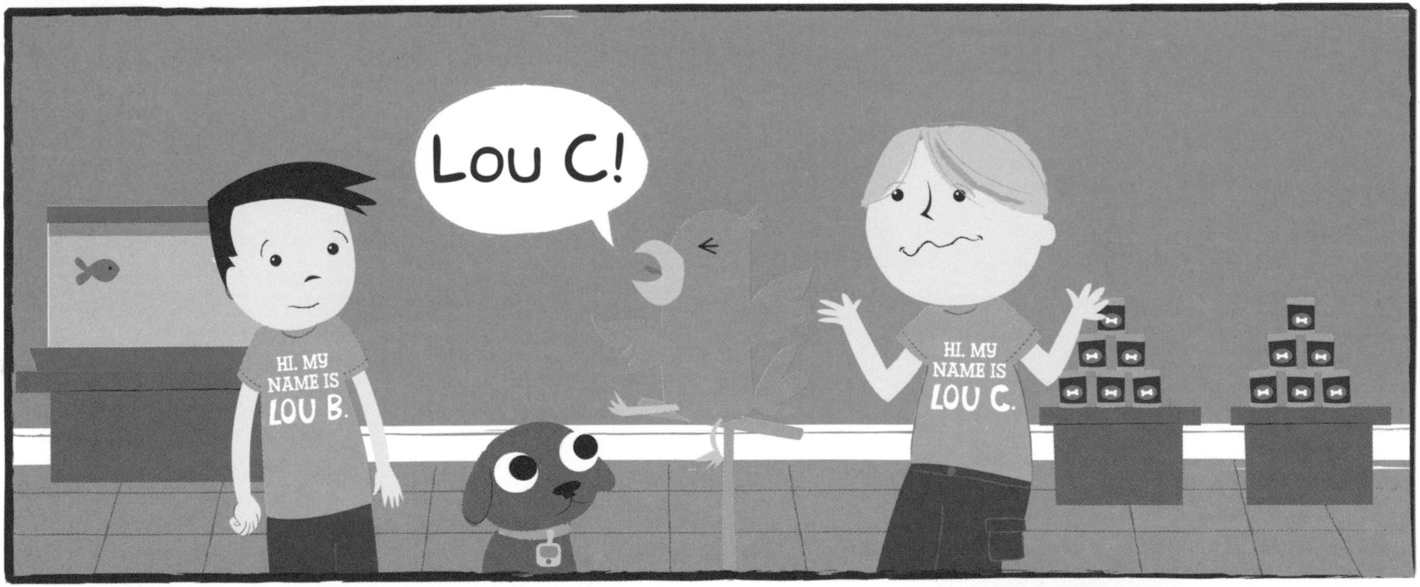
Lou C!
HI. MY NAME IS LOU B.
HI. MY NAME IS LOU C.

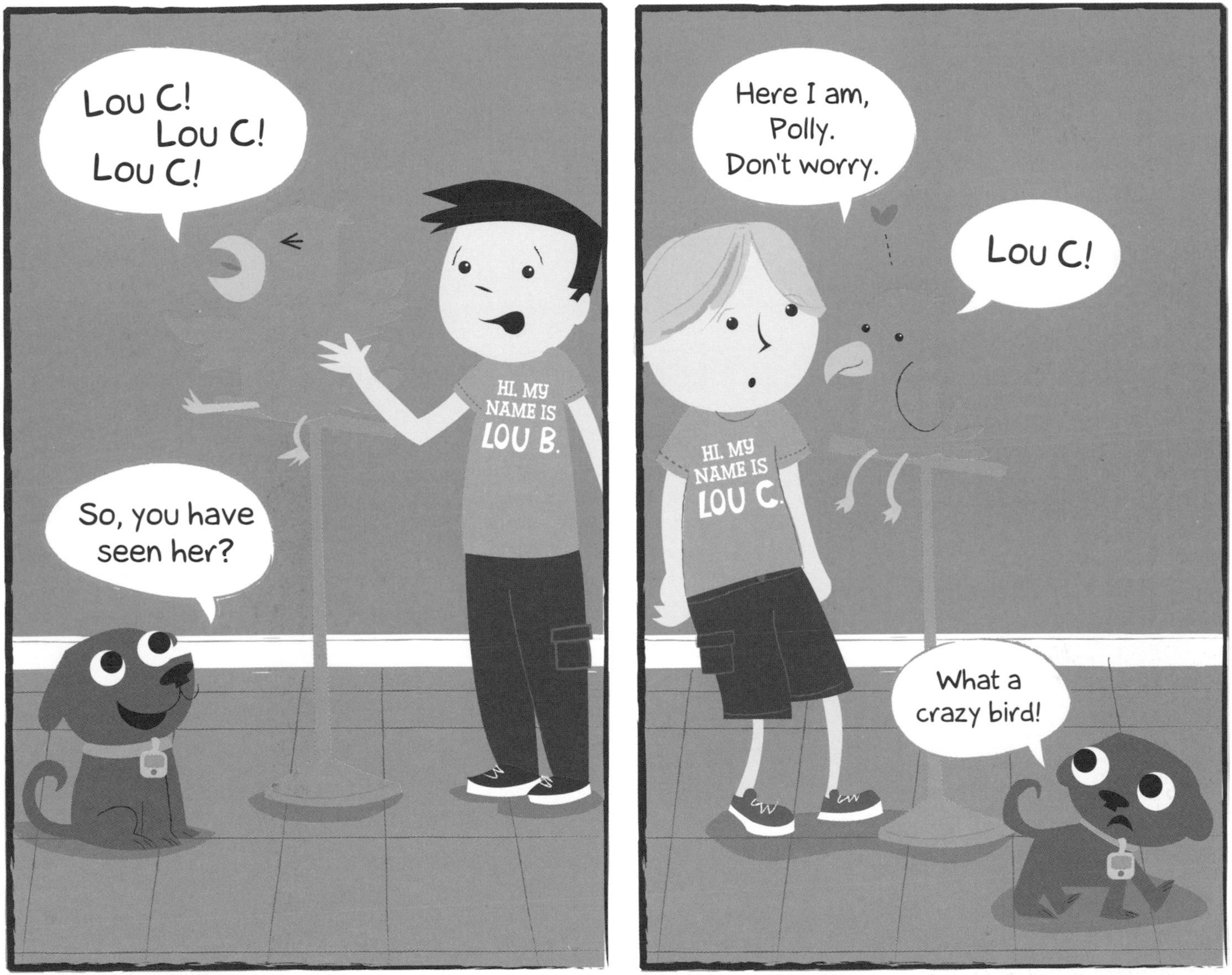
Lou C! Lou C! Lou C!
HI. MY NAME IS LOU B.
So, you have seen her?
Here I am, Polly. Don't worry.
Lou C!
HI. MY NAME IS LOU C.
What a crazy bird!

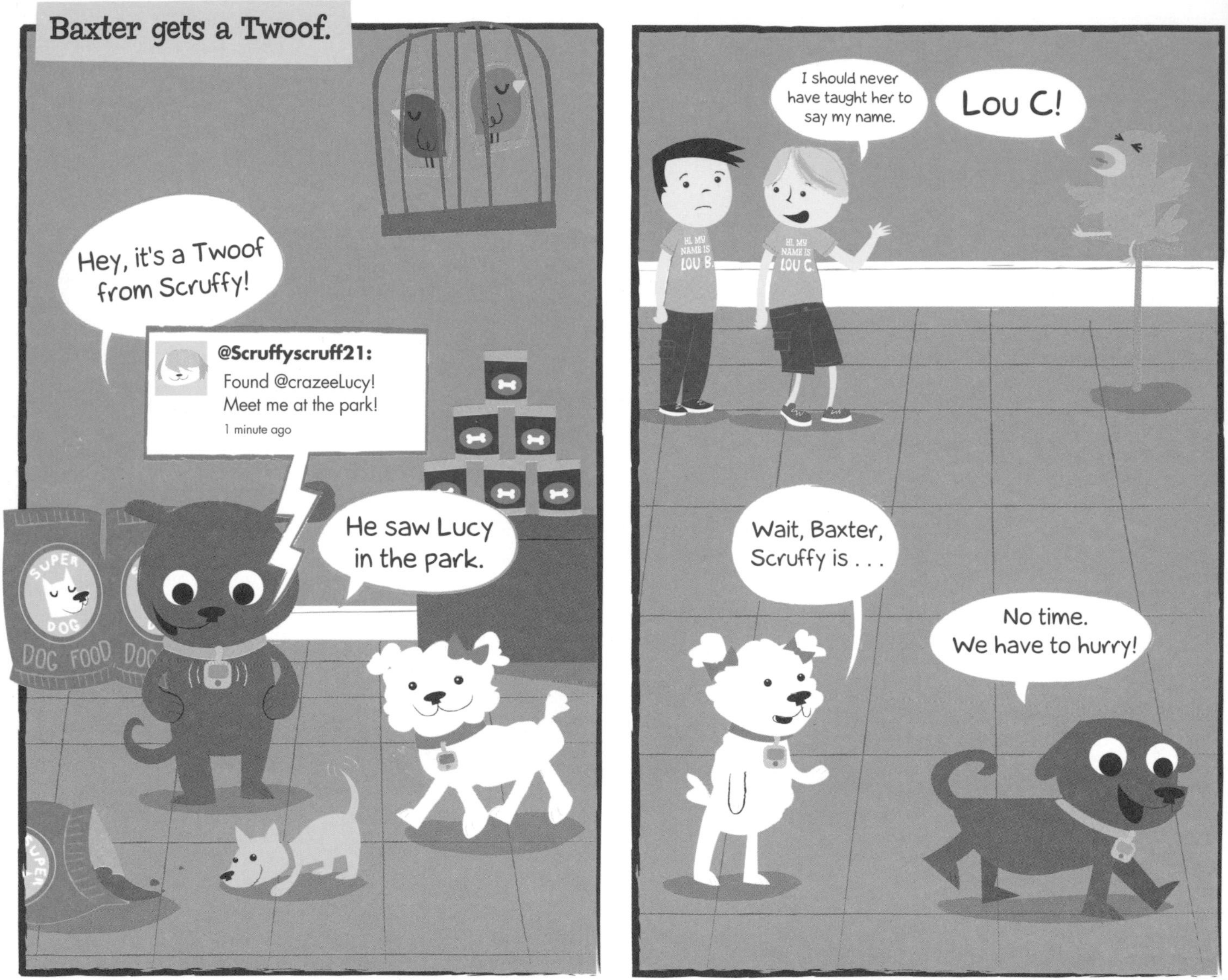
Baxter gets a Twoof.
Hey, it's a Twoof from Scruffy!
@Scruffyscruff21:
Found @crazeeLucy!
Meet me at the park!
1 minute ago
SUPER DOG
DOG FOOD
He saw Lucy in the park.
HI, MY NAME IS LOU B.
HI, MY NAME IS LOU C.
I should never have taught her to say my name.
Lou C!
Wait, Baxter, Scruffy is . . .
No time. We have to hurry!

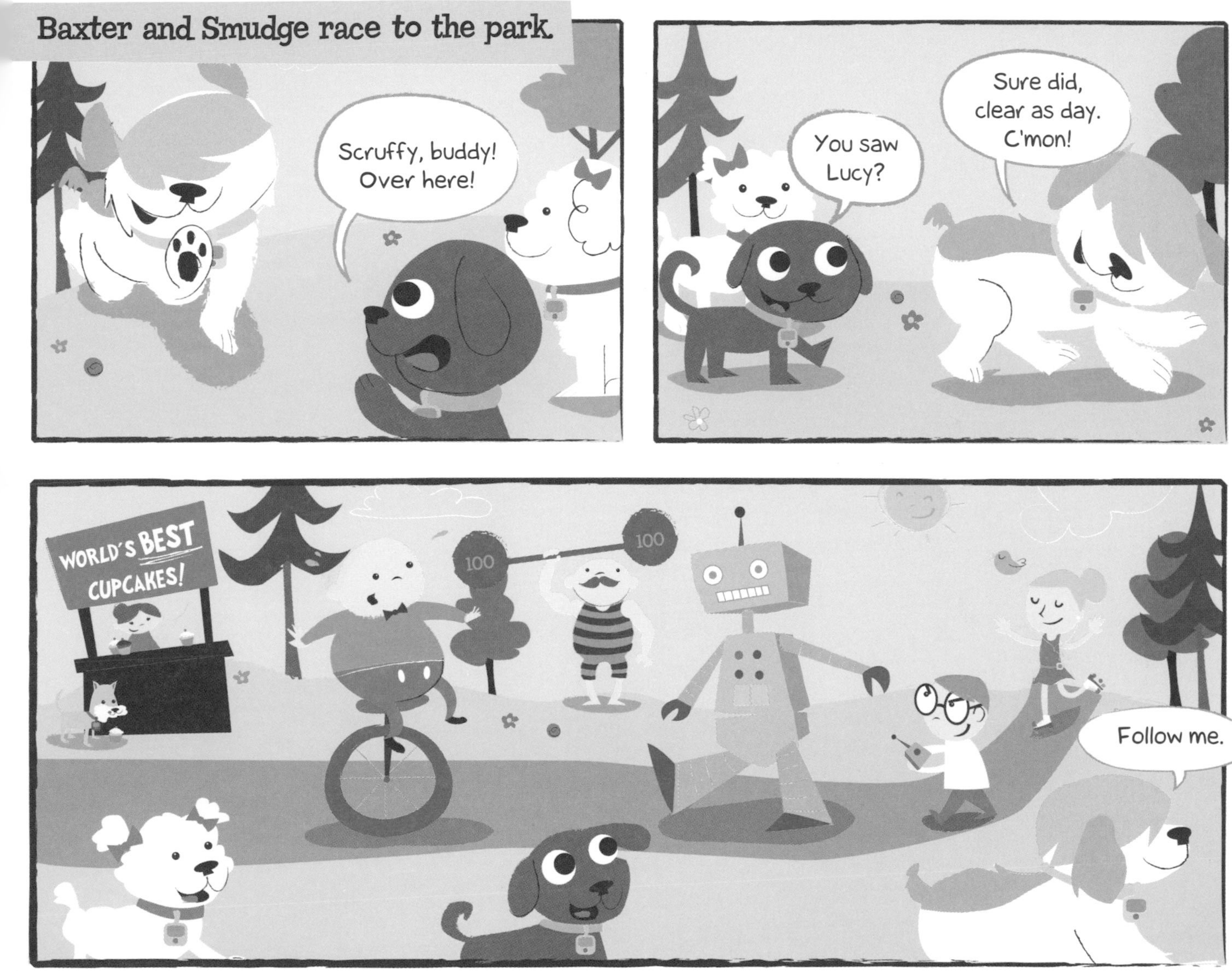
Baxter and Smudge race to the park.
Scruffy, buddy! Over here!
You saw Lucy?
Sure did, clear as day. C'mon!
WORLD'S BEST CUPCAKES!
100
100
Follow me.

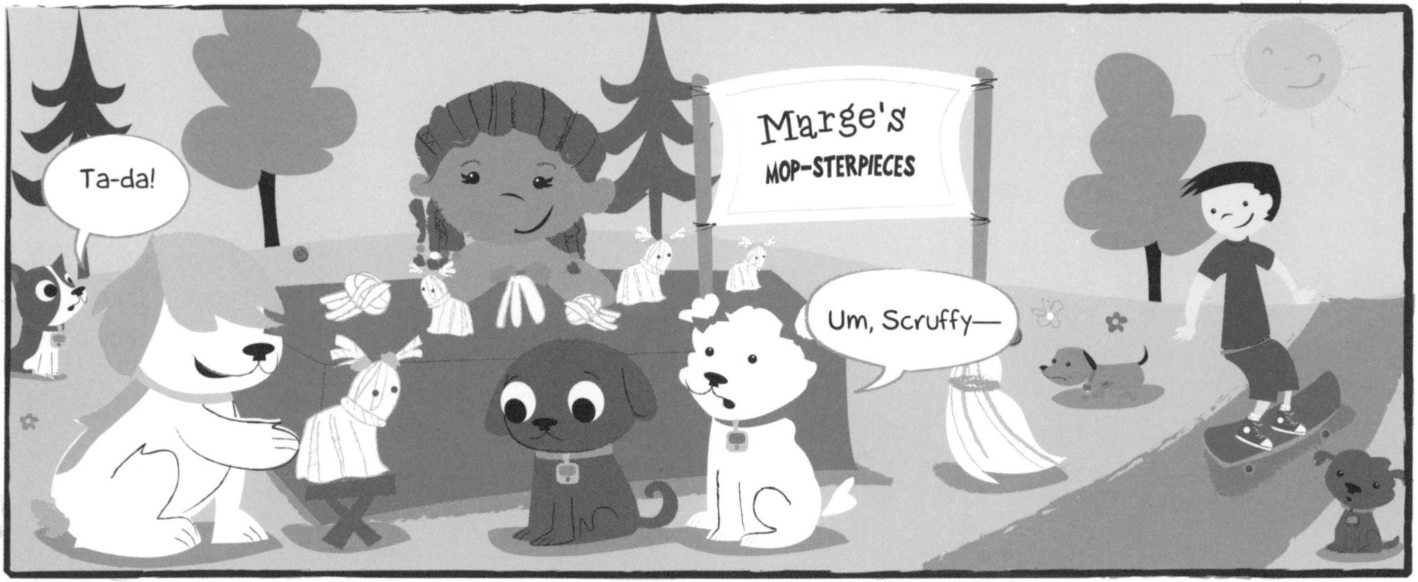
Marge's
MOP-STERPIECES
Ta-da!
Um, Scruffy—

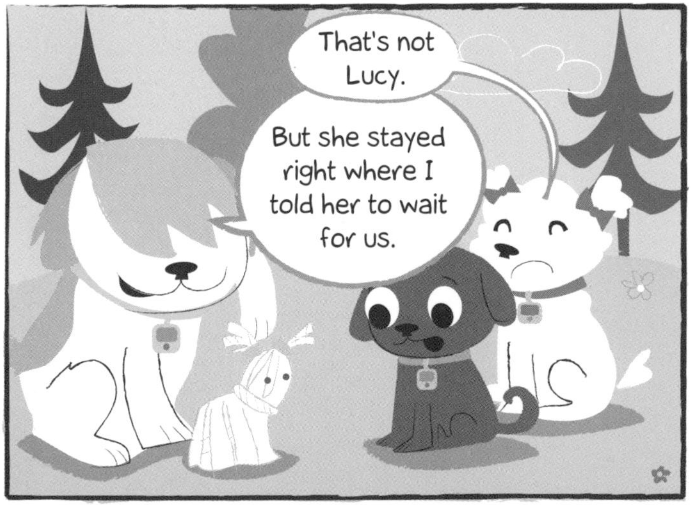
That's not Lucy.
But she stayed right where I told her to wait for us.

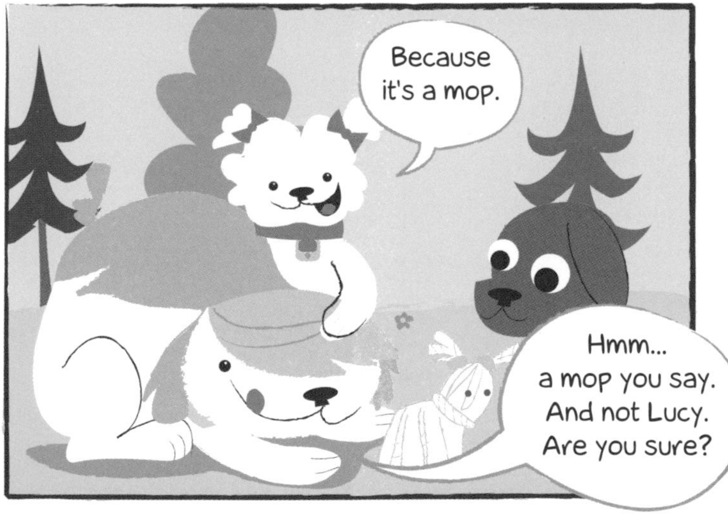
Because it's a mop.
Hmm... a mop you say. And not Lucy. Are you sure?

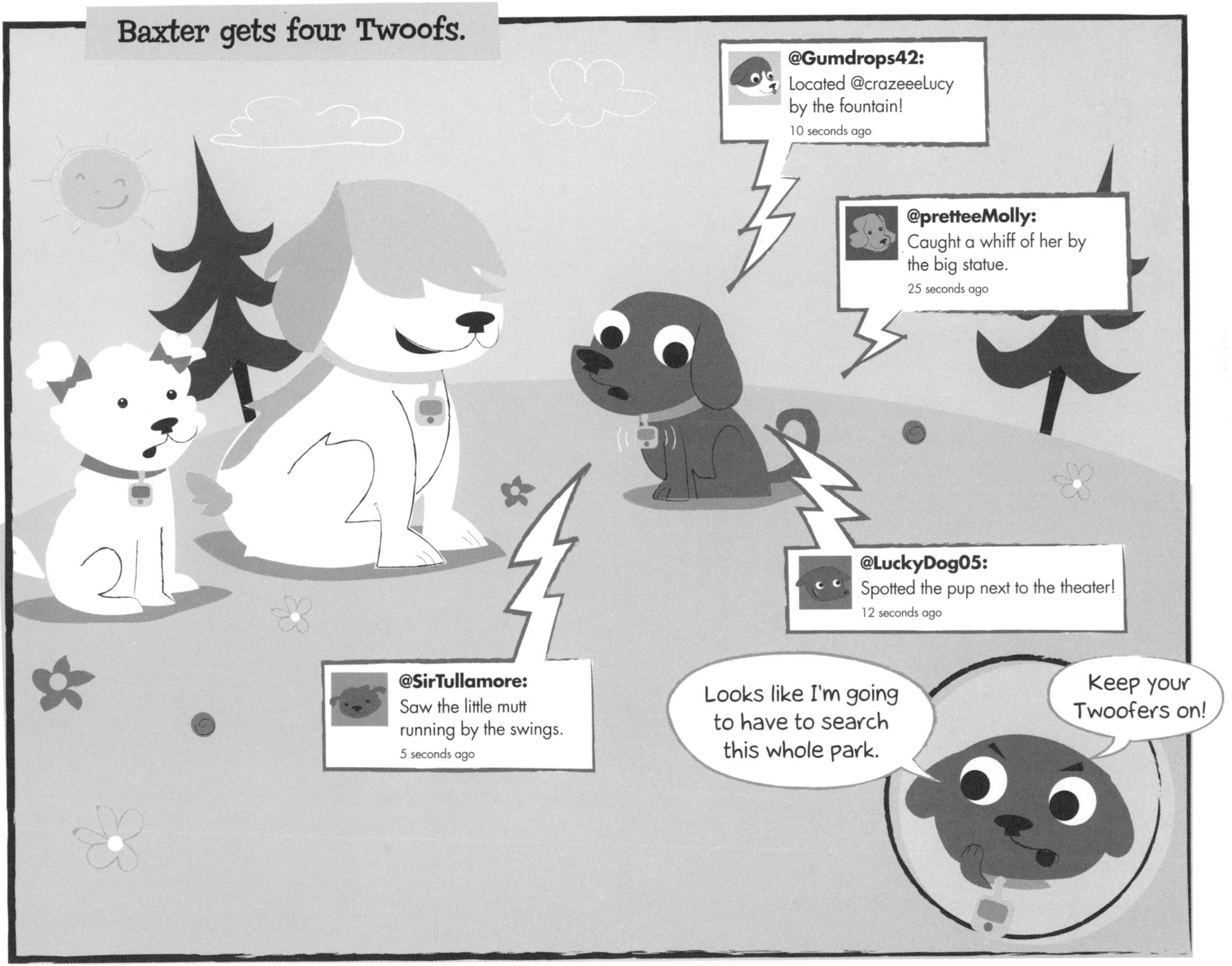
Baxter gets four Twoofs.
@Gumdrops42:
Located @crazeeeLucy by the fountain!
10 seconds ago
@pretteeMolly:
Caught a whiff of her by the big statue.
25 seconds ago
@LuckyDog05:
Spotted the pup next to the theater!
12 seconds ago
@SirTullamore:
Saw the little mutt running by the swings.
5 seconds ago
Looks like I'm going to have to search this whole park.
Keep your Twoofers on!

Baxter searches everywhere for Lucy.

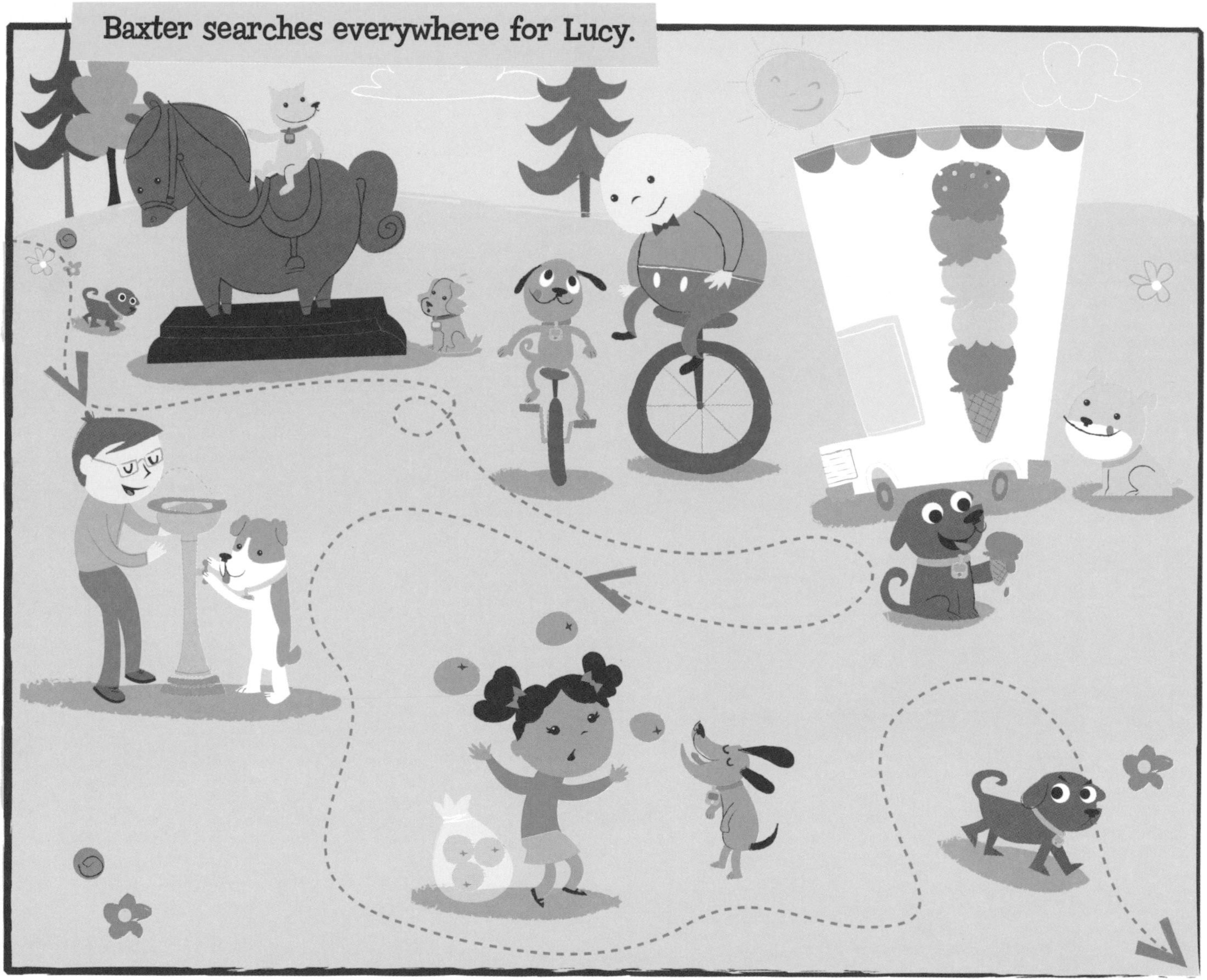

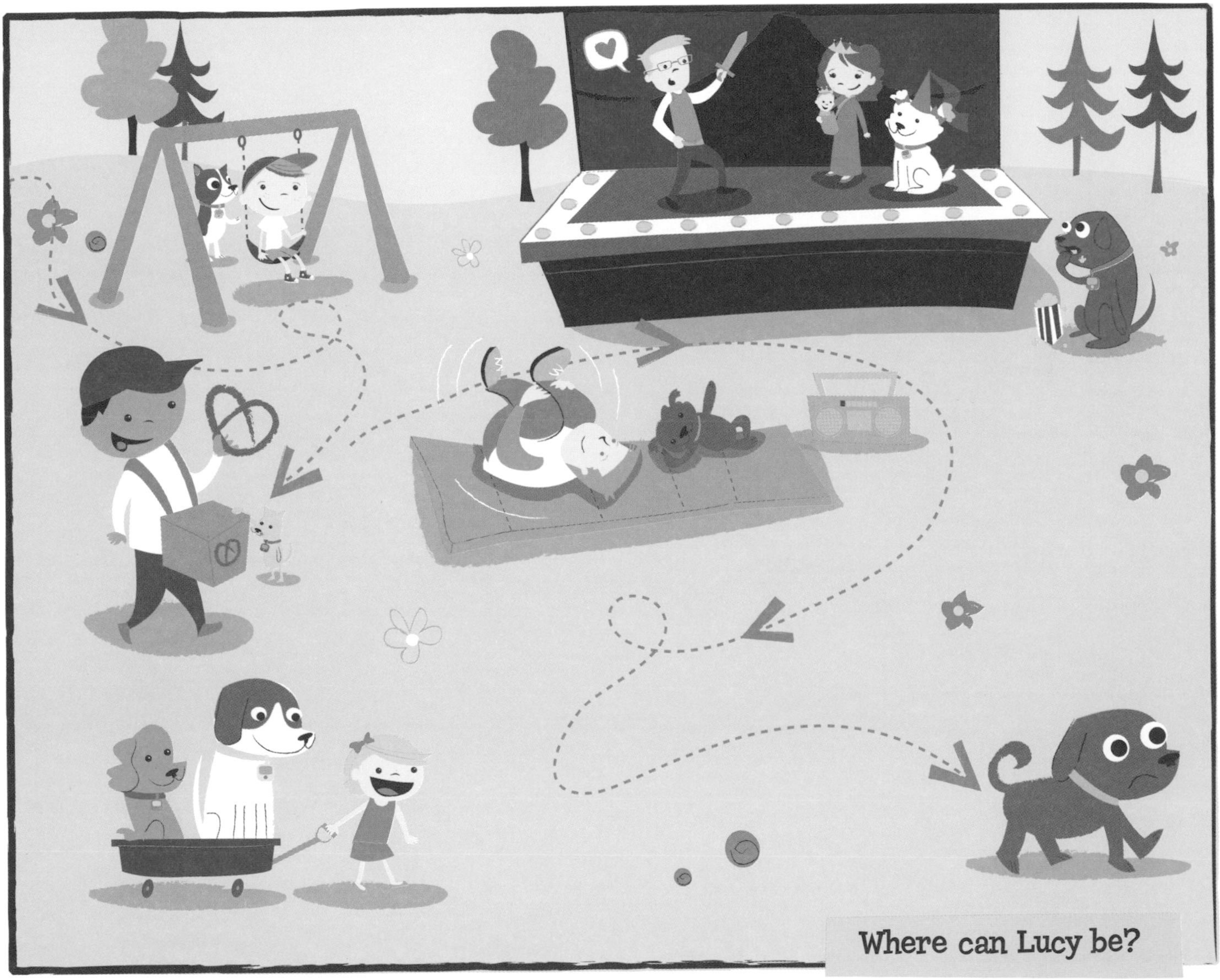

Where can Lucy be?

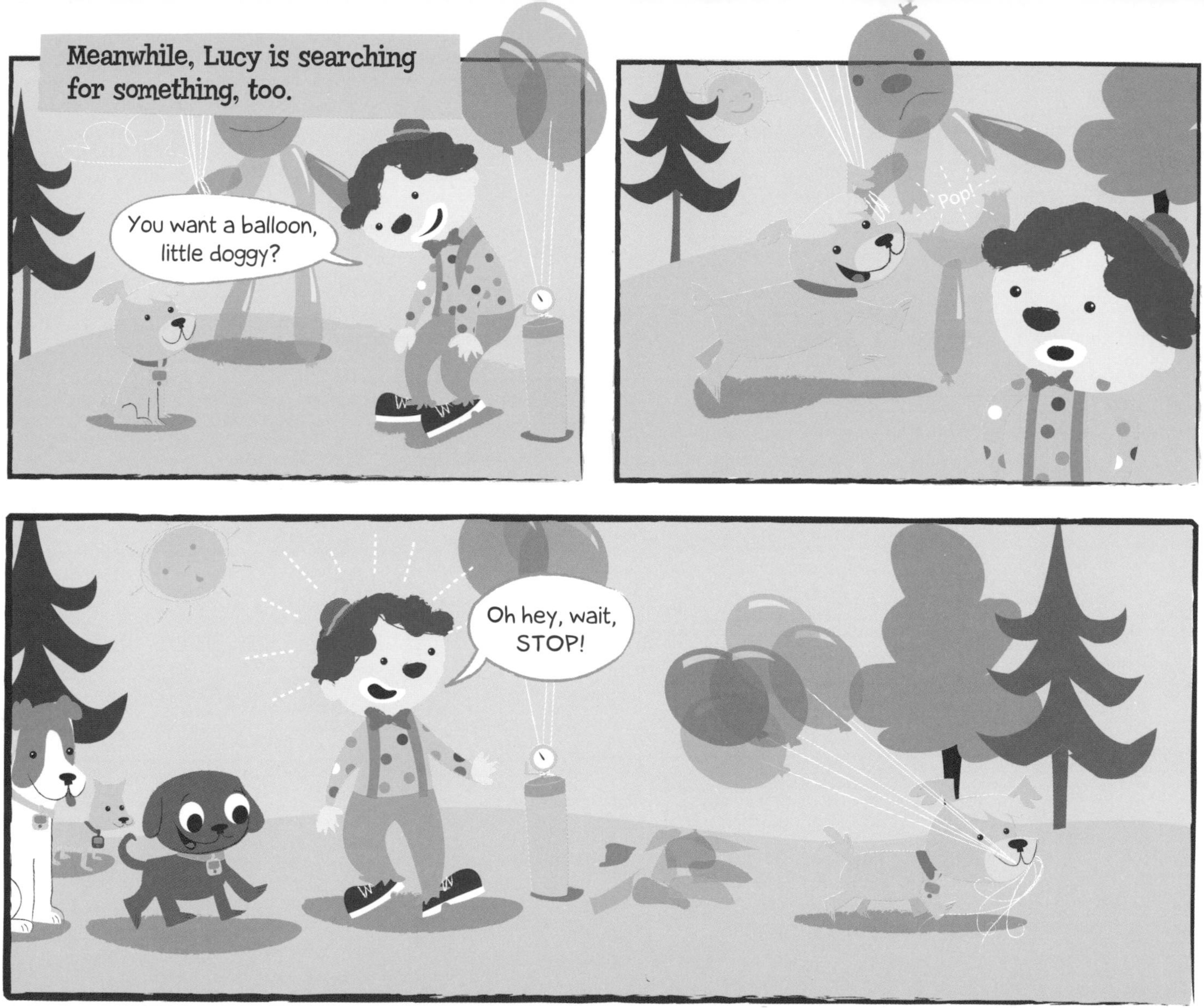
Meanwhile, Lucy is searching for something, too.
You want a balloon, little doggy?
Pop!
Oh hey, wait, STOP!

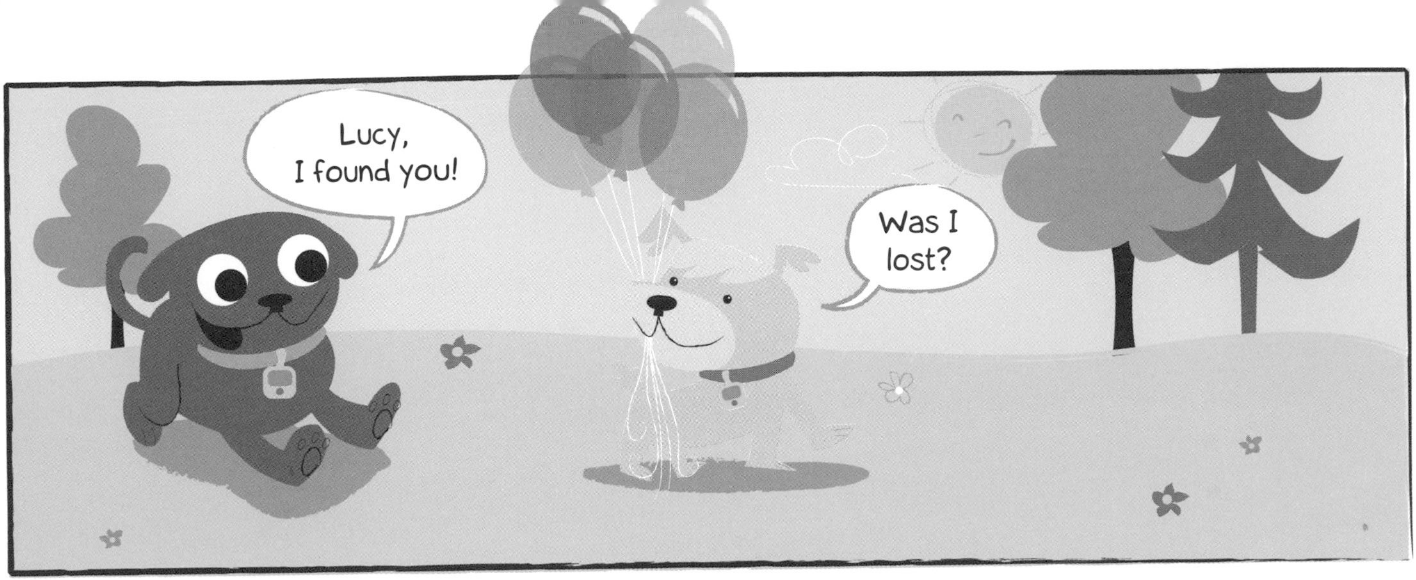
Lucy,
I found you!
Was I
lost?

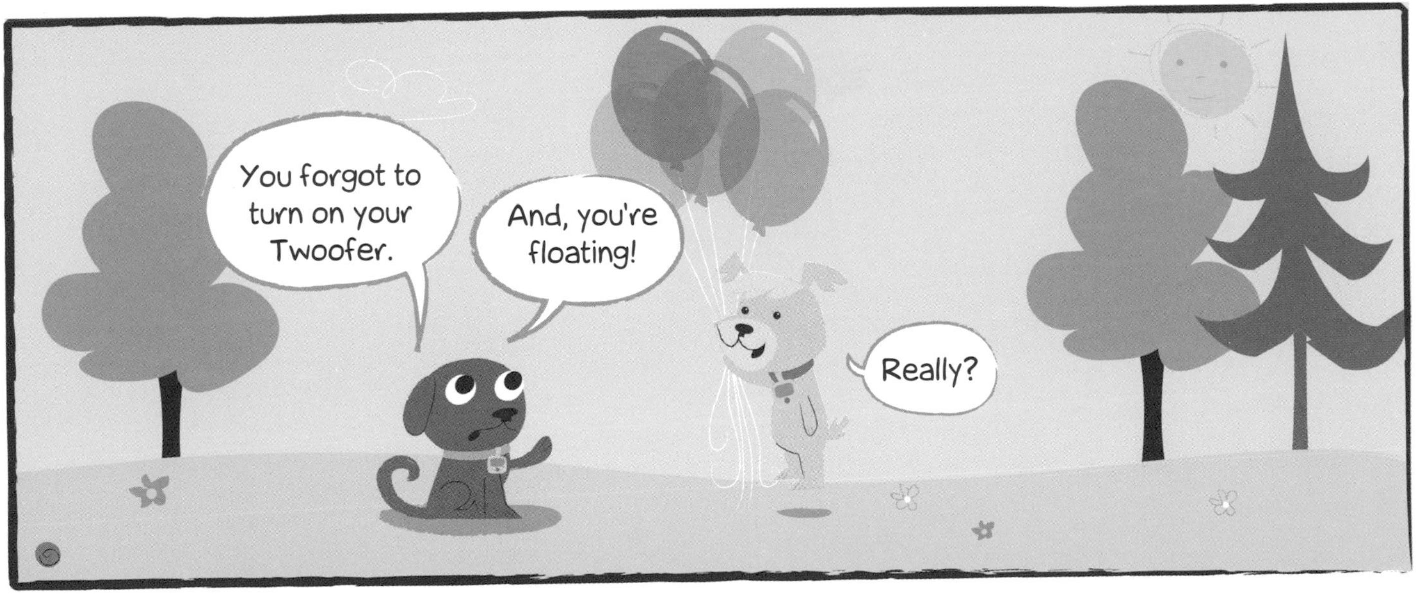
You forgot to
turn on your
Twoofer.
And, you're
floating!
Really?

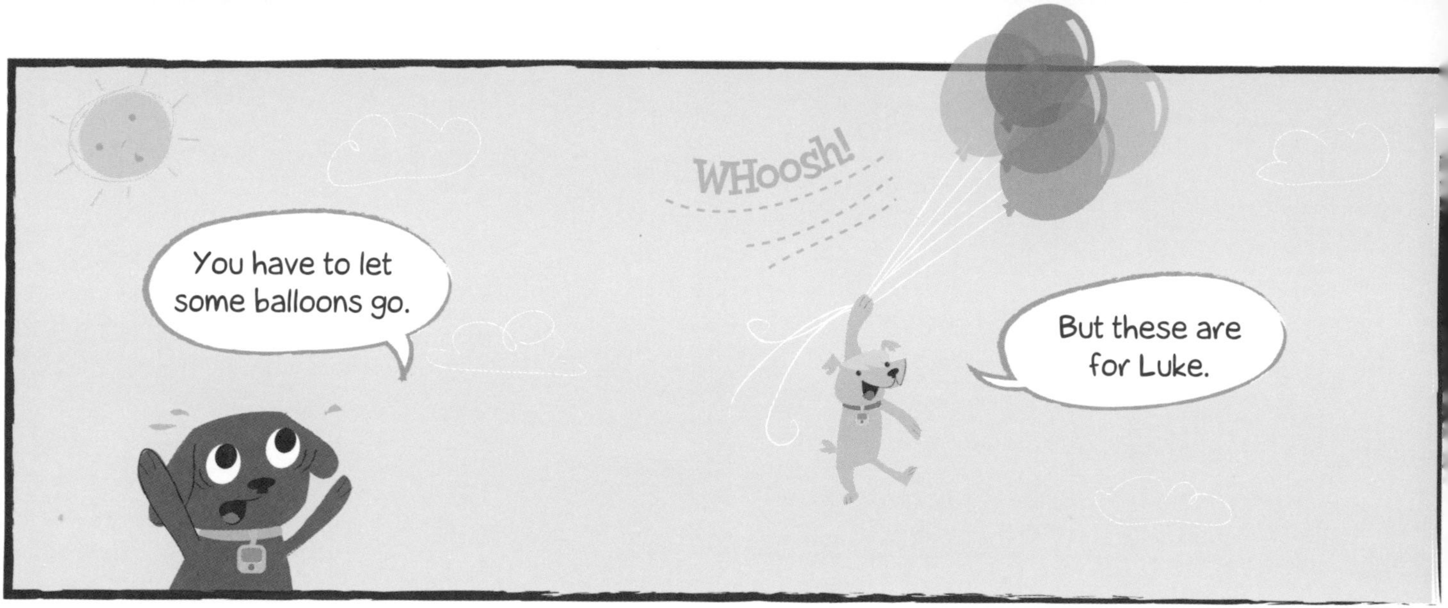
WHoosh!
You have to let some balloons go.
But these are for Luke.

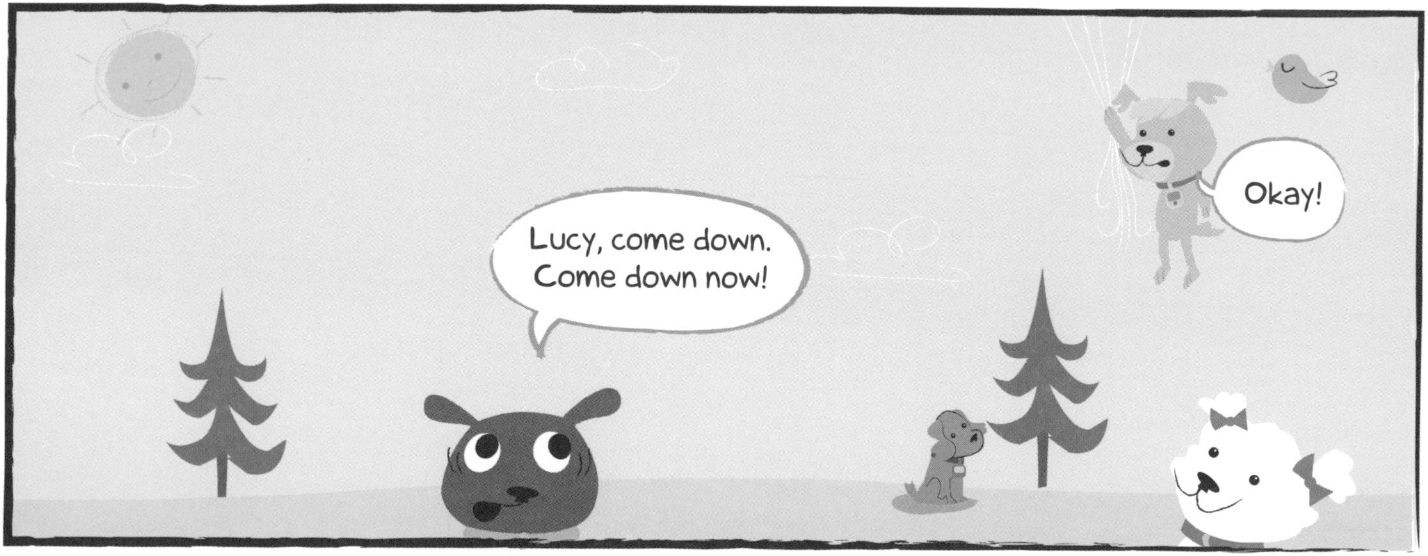
Lucy, come down. Come down now!
Okay!

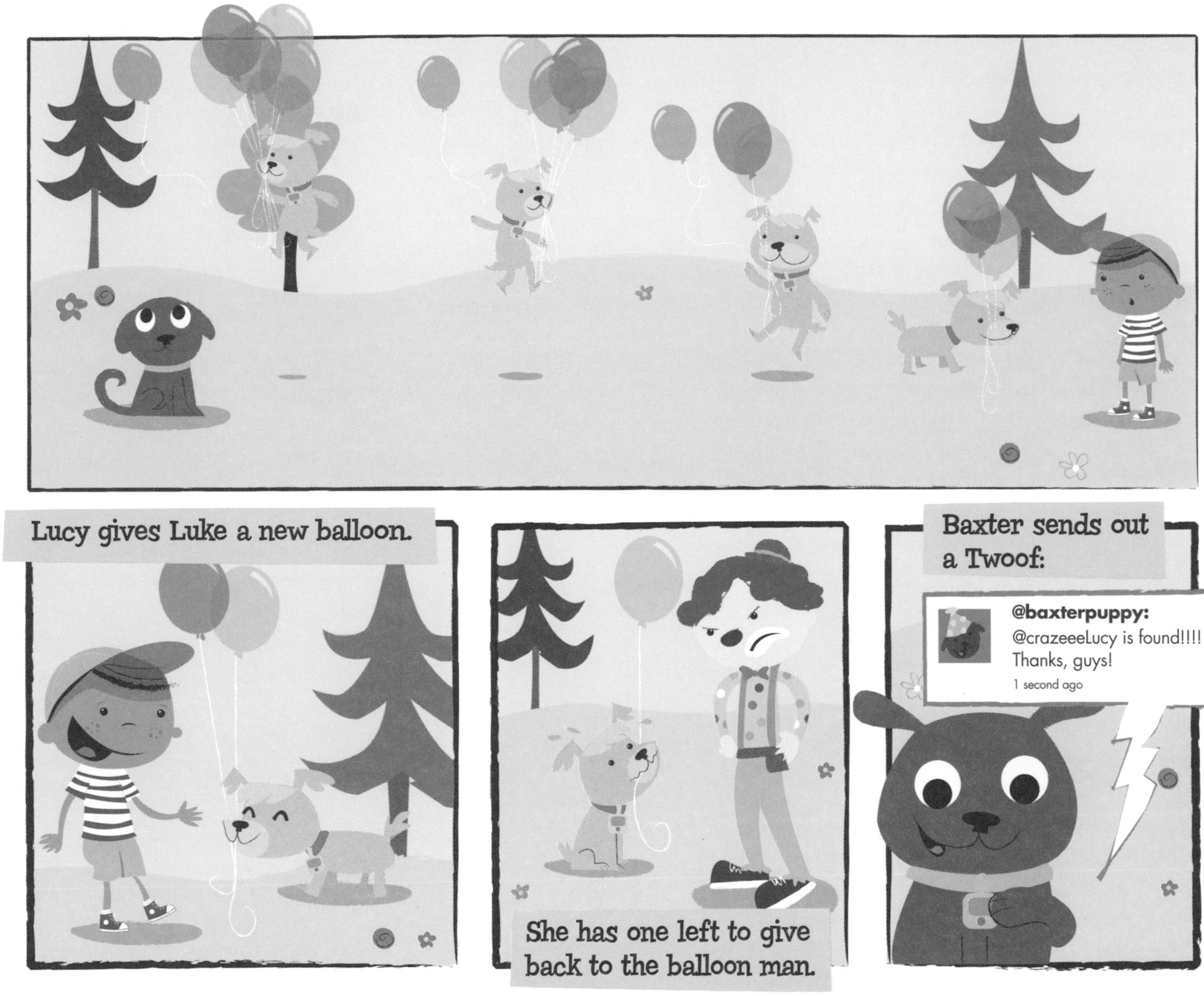
Lucy gives Luke a new balloon.
She has one left to give back to the balloon man.
Baxter sends out a Twoof:
@baxterpuppy:
@crazeeeLucy is found!!!! Thanks, guys!
1 second ago

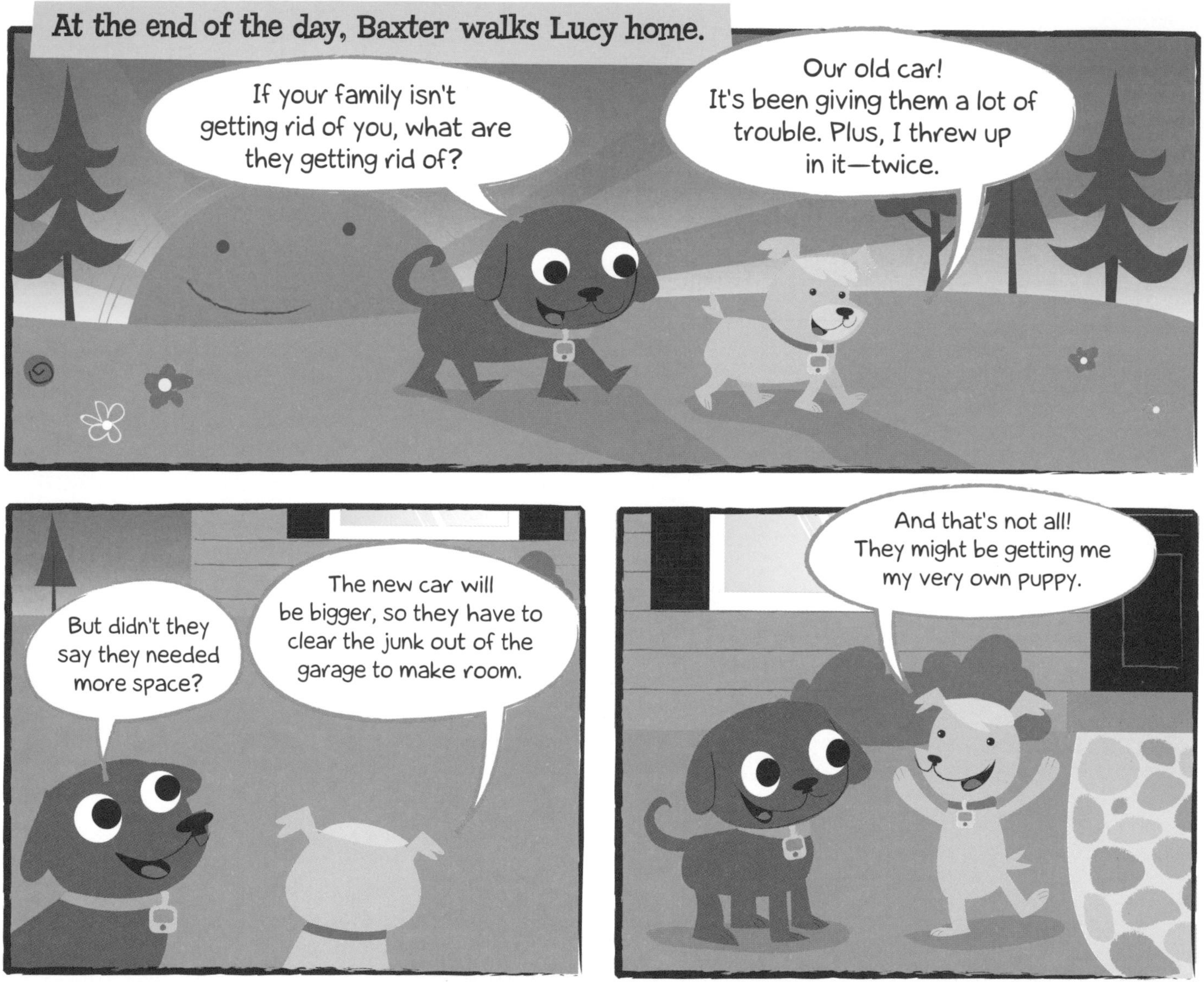
At the end of the day, Baxter walks Lucy home.
If your family isn't getting rid of you, what are they getting rid of?
Our old car! It's been giving them a lot of trouble. Plus, I threw up in it—twice.
But didn't they say they needed more space?
The new car will be bigger, so they have to clear the junk out of the garage to make room.
And that's not all! They might be getting me my very own puppy.

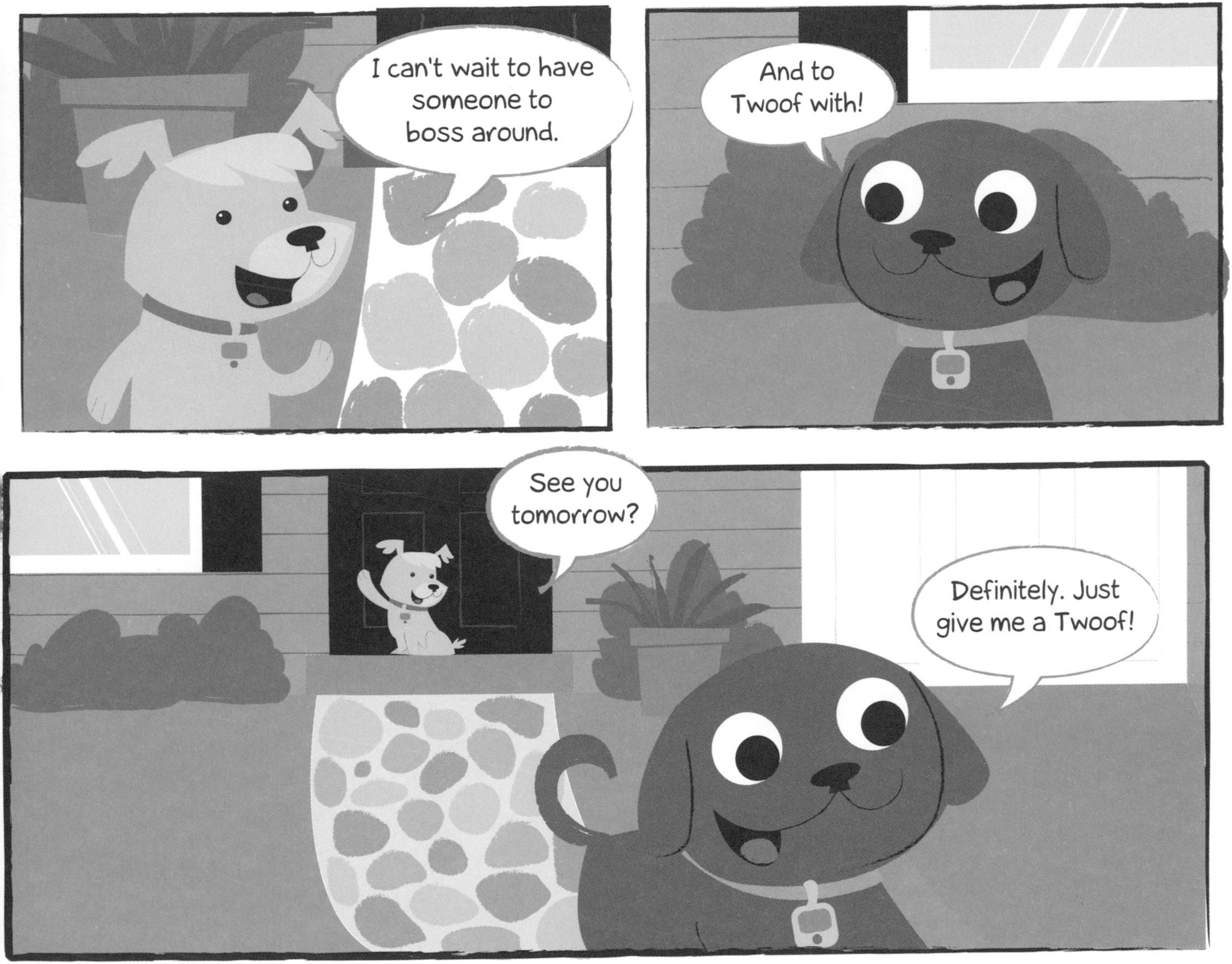
I can't wait to have someone to boss around.
And to Twoof with!
See you tomorrow?
Definitely. Just give me a Twoof!

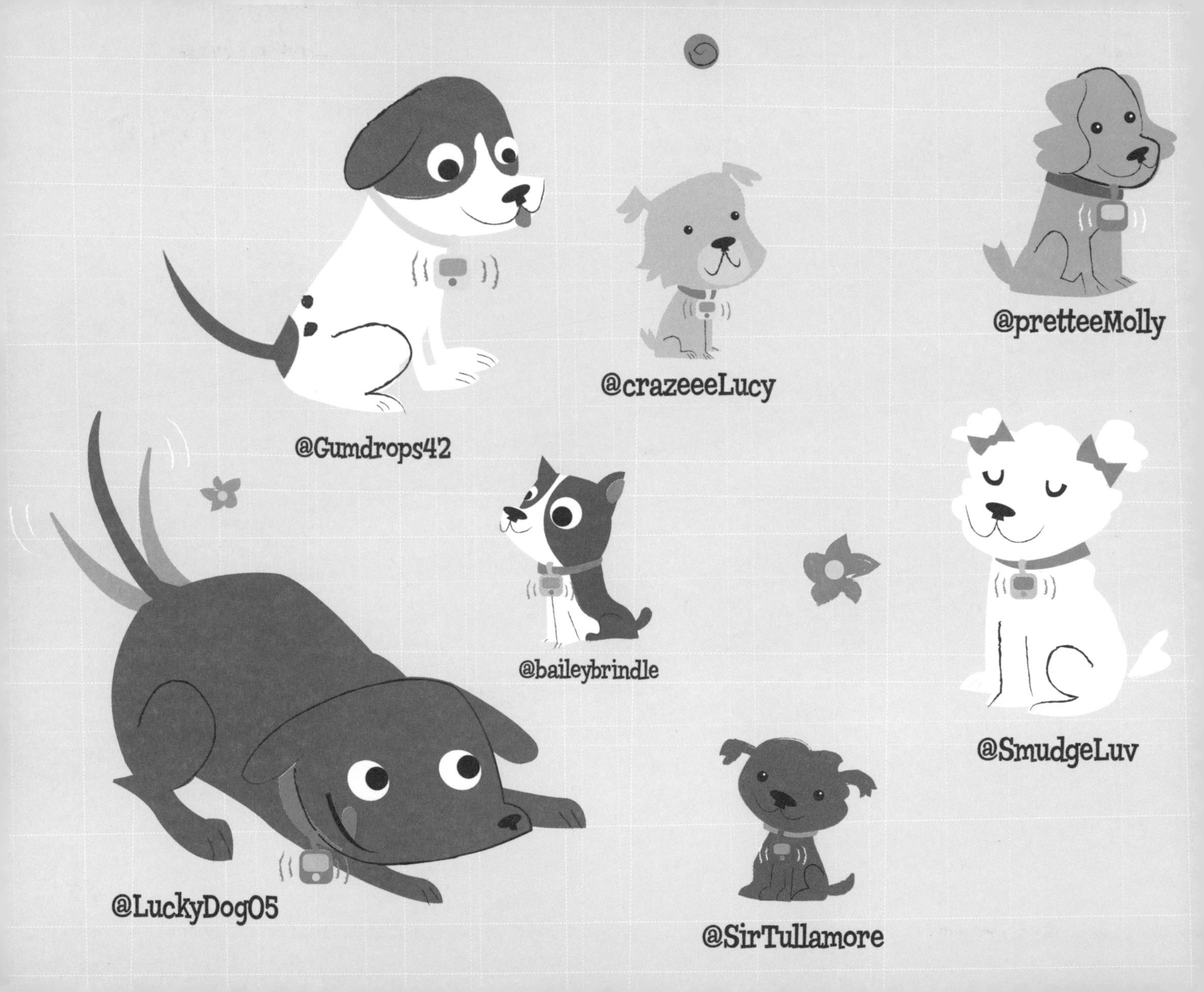

@Gumdrops42
@crazeeeLucy
@pretteeMolly
@baileybrindle
@SmudgeLuv
@LuckyDog05
@SirTullamore